MW01181388

WISHES & TEARS

Copyright © Nancy Loyan Schuemann 2012, 2017
E-book: 978-0-9968956-2-0
Print book: 978-0-9968956-3-7

2nd Edition

All rights reserved. Except for use in any review, the reproduction or utilization of this work in whole or in part in any form by any electronic, mechanical or other means, now known or hereinafter invented, including xerography, photocopying and recording, or in any information storage or retrieval system, is forbidden without the written permission of the publisher.

This is a work of fiction. Names, characters, places and incidents are either the product of the author's imagination or are used fictitiously, and any resemblance to actual persons, living or dead, business establishments, events or locales is entirely coincidental.

Printed in the USA.
Cover Design: Steven Novak

Interior Format

12-1-18

WISHES & TEARS

Love trancends time~

NANCY LOYAN

Love~
Nancy Loyan

ACKNOWLEDGMENTS

I have always been a history buff. Touring historic places, reading about how people lived and amassing books on different episodes of history, historic lifestyles, historic trivia and the like are a passion. When I found a volume written after the Great San Francisco earthquake and fire, I was hooked on the event. It led me to purchase several other historic accounts of this tragic moment in United States history.

Then, I had a dream. It was a dream about a handsome doctor practicing in San Francisco during that historic time period. The "what if?" that writers think of popped into my mind and wouldn't leave. It led me to research medicine of the time period and lifestyles. My imagination took over and this novel was born.

This novel would have never been published were it not for the supportive writers' critique group I had been a member of for a number of years. Though we split after our busy lives as published authors took hold, I am forever grateful for their influence and input.

I want to thank members Mary Ann Chulick, Christine Nolfi, Christy Carlson, Dianne Kodger Harper, Ellen Deely, Debby Johnson and the late Ruth Nelson for helping me become the published writer I am today. I would be remiss in not acknowledging my past critique partners, Al Chaput and the late great June Lund Shiplet as well. June, by the way, created the romance time travel genre with her novel, Journey to Yesterday.

A special thank you to my readers, for having "faith" in me!

Dedicated to my fellow writers.
The struggle is worth it.

PROLOGUE 2006

"*I DON'T LOVE YOU ANYMORE. I want a divorce," Brad said, his voice devoid of emotion and remorse.*

Faith sat in stunned silence at the turn the morning conversation had taken. First, he said that he didn't love her. Now, the words a woman never wants to hear. What went wrong? Love and commitment had suddenly been replaced with guilt and betrayal.

"There's something you should know. You know Pamela at the firm?" Brad asked, looking up from his mug of strong black coffee. His eyes, once his most vibrant feature, were dark and vacant when they met hers.

"Yes." Faith choked on a lump forming in her throat, fearful of what he might say next. Pamela was the new perky blonde associate at his firm, bright and curvaceous. Just out of Harvard Law School, hadn't he interviewed her for the job?

"She's expecting my baby. We're getting married," he said bluntly.

Remembering his words made her tremble. He had the audacity to have a baby with someone else!

For fifteen years Faith had sacrificed and struggled to help him build a comfortable life. Now that he was partner in the law firm, now that they owned a stately home and could afford the freedom and luxuries money could buy, he wanted to tear it all apart.

Ever since her freshman year in college, Faith had done everything for Brad from typing his papers to doing his laundry. When they married after graduation, she had given up her own dreams of law school for him. Instead, she taught school to support his ambition. She agreed to forsake her family and friends and move across the country to fulfill Brad's desire to live and work in San Francisco. She even agreed to sacrifice motherhood when he made it clear he didn't want to be burdened with children.

When Faith shared the news at dinner tonight, her best friend Clarice had been floored. Everyone in their circle thought that Brad and Faith had a marriage to be admired and envied. Brad was always sending her roses at work with sexy little notes. They were always holding hands and cuddling like newlyweds. The way they gazed into each other's eyes was so electric they seemed lost in their own romantic world even when in a crowd.

"How could a love like yours, one that seemed so perfect, die without anyone knowing?" Clarice asked.

Faith certainly hadn't seen it coming.

Faith had spilled out her soul so much she had hardly eaten, and the glass of Chardonnay had done little to calm her nerves. Clarice had listened, tried to be encouraging, pledged her support, and had hugged her in a sympathetic embrace before leaving the restaurant.

Faith drew a deep breath. Clarice was now en route to her home, to a husband and children. Faith wondered how she, herself, could face an empty house and an empty life.

"Brad, you bastard!" she screamed, the words echoing off the wood veneer dash and leather upholstery. "How can I start over after wasting the best years of my life with you?"

She gazed out the windshield. From the hilltop parking space she could see the lights of the city twinkling below. The expanse of the Golden Gate Bridge was silhouetted against a moonlit sky as the fog began to blanket the calm bay. She sniffled, dabbing the tears from her cheeks with trembling fingers.

After wiping the last stray tear, she turned the key in the ignition. With her other hand, she maneuvered the stick shift while depressing the clutch. As she moved her foot to the gas pedal, the car lurched forward rather than the intended reverse. Instead of backing out of the parking space, her car sped forward. Realizing her mistake, she shifted into reverse but it was too late.

Faith gasped in horror as she realized her loss of control. As if in slow motion, the red Jaguar was airborne, gliding on air currents as it sailed into the darkness over the hilltop where it had been parked. In numb disbelief, she clung to the steering wheel as the Jaguar began its dive. She felt the blood draining from her fingers, knuckles, and face. She could see downtown San Francisco aglow with life and the streamers of headlights crowding the Golden Gate Bridge. For a moment she was suspended in a peaceful, ethereal sky.

"Oh my God, I'm gonna die! I'm gonna die!" she repeated over and over, the words strangled in her throat as the automobile descended into darkness.

She closed her eyes. Visions of her life flashed before her like a tape, fast- forwarding through scenes. The good times seemed to be highlighted as if to bring peace and calm in reflection. *Is this what it feels like to die?*

The impact of steel hitting water jolted her back against her seat with such force she was left breathless. She wheezed for air as the car floated on the misty surface of the glossy bay. She tried to regain her composure. After unbuckling her seatbelt she pressed the buttons to open the car windows but the wiring had already short–circuited. She pulled at the door handles but they wouldn't budge. As the sleek car began its descent into the murky depths, she let out a shrill scream. Soon, the chilled wet began to seep into the car as the water began to rise outside, engulfing her. She urged herself to remain calm and to think if she didn't want to drown in the sealed tomb of her car… if she didn't want to die.

As the water enveloped the interior of her car, she crawled up toward the inside roof for air, remembering that it would be the last air pocket. She fumbled for the door handle. Hadn't she read about doors opening if the water pressure was equalized both inside and out? Taking a last deep breath, she reached down under water and tugged at the door handle. To her relief, the door popped open. Groping her way, she squeezed out into the rush of water. She followed the instinct of her body's desire to float upward and swim up through the darkness.

After what seemed like an eternity, she broke the water's surface. Her chest heaved as she gasped for breath. After drawing the crisp night air into her lungs she was renewed. Faith treaded water and opened her eyes. Only the moonlight and a sky sprinkled with stars shone over her, the mist, and the stillness of the glassy water. The night was quiet, eerily quiet. She was so completely alone. What a fitting ending to the darkest day of her life.

CHAPTER 1

FAITH AWAKENED NESTLED IN THE warmth of a flannel nightgown and downy comfort of a bed in a room that felt oddly familiar. Her lips formed a thin smile as she thought that the episode with Brad and her prized car sinking into the bay was nothing more than a bad dream. As she opened her eyes, though, a shiver of foreboding penetrated her body.

Confused, she surveyed the room. The intricate, stained glass window in the dormer, the finely chiseled millwork of the ceiling moldings, and the buffed parquet floor were identical to those in her bedroom at home. The furnishings, though, were not her own. Instead of the brass and glass she had purchased with Brad, fine Victorian pieces decorated the room. She scooted up in a bed created of white enamel baked on iron, trimmed and ornamented in shiny brass. Along the perimeter of the room were a tall rosewood wardrobe, matching dresser, and chiffonier. A commode held a porcelain toilet set and crisp linen towels. The carved mantel framed a glowing hearth that helped to illuminate the room while a Tiffany lamp set on a bedside table assisted. She looked up at the gilt–framed mirror that hung above the mantel and across at a nearby wicker chair set.

Tapestry draperies covered the long, narrow windows and a Persian rug accented the floor. She thought the room was an impressive reproduction of a past era but wondered where she was and how she had ended up here.

Before she could gather her thoughts, the door to the bedroom opened. A maid attired in a vintage uniform waddled into the room carrying a wicker bed tray set with a china tea service. She approached the bed where Faith lay and gently set the tray down upon it.

Faith glanced up from the maid to the tea service and back up at the maid.

"The tea with honey will be good for you, ma'am, to warm your body and chase away the fever and chills," the maid said in a thick Irish brogue. She smiled a kindly but crooked smile and curtsied.

"Thank you," Faith answered, analyzing the woman's round face, ruddy complexion, and sparkling blue eyes.

"If you need anything, just ring the bell on your nightstand and I'll scurry up to help."

"Who are you?" Faith asked.

The maid tilted her head meeting Faith's confused gaze. "I'm Bridget, ma'am, and my orders are to take good care of you."

"Your orders? I don't understand."

"Doctor Forrester, ma'am. He's my employer, a fine man, and he asked me to watch over you. That's what I've been doing since he brought you home the evening last."

"He brought me to his home?" Faith eased herself up in an erect sitting position. The little exertion winded her and made the room spin. She put her hand to her forehead, closing her eyes.

"Let me help you. You're not well." Bridget leaned over the bed. She fluffed the goose-down pillows before rearranging them behind Faith to support her head and neck.

"I feel like hell," Faith said, drawing her other hand up to her forehead where a headache was beginning to throb.

Bridget smirked. "Fever and chills. Scanty wet clothes on a cold evening will do it every time. No telling how long you were lying on the banks of the bay before he found you."

"Who found me?" Faith opened her eyes. The banks of the bay?

"Doctor Forrester, ma'am. He's always going out of his way to help those that are destitute and in need." Bridget took the china teapot and poured some of the steaming brew into the china cup. She handed the full cup on a saucer to Faith.

With trembling fingers, Faith accepted the delicate cup and saucer. She lifted the cup up to her lips and sipped the fine English tea steeped with honey. After taking another sip, she asked, "Where am I?"

"In Pacific Heights."

"That's funny. I live in Pacific Heights, 92 Sacramento Street to be exact."

Bridget wrinkled her brow and answered, "That isn't possible, ma'am. This is 92 Sacramento Street."

"What are you saying?"

"This is 92 Sacramento. Doctor Forrester built this home and is the only one who resides here."

"Is this some sort of joke?" Faith set down the cup and saucer on the bed tray.

"No, ma'am."

"Get me a telephone and we'll clear this up," Faith demanded. Her head was beginning to pound but she disregarded the pain. All she wanted were answers.

"Telephone?"

"Don't look so perplexed. Just get me a phone." She had to call Clarice, to call someone.

"The doctor's telephone is downstairs in his office. You're in no condition—"

Faith cut her off. "What kind of doctor is he? Doesn't he have a cordless phone, a cellular phone? Something?"

The pain in her head was becoming excruciating. Being upset was making it unbearable. Faith cradled her aching head in her hands as tears of anguish swelled in her eyes. She couldn't speak but softly moaned.

Bridget turned and rushed out of the room in a panic. Faith watched her leave, hoping that the maid was getting a phone. Home was only a phone call away.

When the door to the bedroom opened, a man instead of the maid entered. Faith glanced up at him through tears and splayed fingers. His height and attire made for a striking appearance. The black tuxedo with tails seemed a bit dated. The black cape thrown over his shoulder and the black silk top hat he held made him appear ready for a costume ball. Yet, the strange attire seemed to fit his arrogant demeanor and erect stance. Faith stared at him as he strode toward her. He returned her gaze with like curiosity.

"It seems I've returned home from the theater just in time. Bridget informed me of your being conscious and in some discomfort," he said in a dusky voice. "I'm Doctor Ian Forrester."

With the flair of a matador, he removed his cape and set it and the hat upon the nearby wicker chair. He came to her bedside and looked down at her, concern flickering gold in his dark chocolate eyes. He leaned over and placed his right hand on her forehead and moved it down to her cheeks and throat. His long fingers were soft and gentle against her flesh, the fingers one expected from a facialist or masseur.

"You're still burning with fever," he said, removing his hands. "When the fever goes down your headache will be less pronounced. In the meantime, I can mix up some medicine to lessen the pain."

"Don't you have any Tylenol or Advil?" she asked.

"I don't understand."

"You are a doctor, aren't you?" she asked, flustered.

"I assure you that I am and I've been told I'm a competent one."

His gaze was intense as he analyzed her every word and movement. Faith squirmed under the quilt and sheets.

"You really must rest. Getting upset will only delay your recovery," he said. "You should tell me your name and if there is someone I should inform about your condition and your whereabouts."

"My name is Faith Donahue and I would like to call my friend."

"Telephone?"

"Yes. Bridget said that you have one."

"Since you cannot leave your bed, allow me to place your telephone call."

"Okay." She sighed. "The name is Clarice Thomas. She's in SOMA and her number is five–five–eight–four–three–two–four."

"Madame, I don't understand."

"What is there to understand?"

"I know of no such a place as SOMA and the exchange isn't valid."

Faith raised her hands. "Where am I, on another planet?"

"San Francisco can seem that way." He chuckled. "Perhaps your illness has caused some confusion. You really should rest."

"The only place I can rest is at home."

"And where's that?"

"92 Sacramento Street in Pacific Heights."

He chuckled again. "Are you trying to humor me? This is 92 Sacramento Street and this is my home."

"What kind of joke is this? Brad put you up to this charade, didn't he? He wants me declared insane so he can get his divorce without losing his assets. Admit it!"

"Madame, I don't know who you are or where you come from. All I do know is that I found you near death on the banks of San Francisco Bay. Out of duty I brought you here. I'm afraid that I can only cure the physical. I am not a doctor who deals with illnesses of the psyche."

He shook his head as if in pity of her state of mind. With a turn of heels, he marched across and out of the room.

The powdery substance that Doctor Forrester had mixed was working wonders on Faith's fever and headache. Before, all she wished to do was to be left alone to sleep. Sleep had been her only escape from the sharp pain in her head, the nausea, and lethargy. After the medicine and Bridget's attentive care, she was regaining her strength. As she began to feel better, a desire for independence set in.

Instead of being a refuge, the bed was becoming a prison. Her curiosity about the strange house and its unusual occupants was growing on her. She also wanted to call Clarice, go home, and plan for her future without Brad.

After Bridget set down her morning tea and left, Faith scooted to the edge of her bed. She let her legs and feet dangle for a while to get the blood circulating again. Feeling confident, she stood on her wobbly legs, grasping the iron headboard for support. Her legs were numb and weak and her mind a bit foggy. With determination she moved one foot in front of the other, reaching the iron footboard. She stood clinging to the iron post, contemplating her next move.

The sun was radiating through the stained glass creating a colorful, fiery effect. Tapestry draperies were pulled over the other two windows keeping the room dim. Faith decided that she needed some sunlight and fresh air.

Releasing her hold on the footboard, she gingerly stepped toward a window. After drawing open the heavy drapes, she sank into a nearby chair. Winded, she drew a deep breath and opened her eyes to the world outside her window. She gasped at the scene below. Something was wrong, terribly wrong.

The scene outside was like some Hollywood movie set. She reached out and pushed up the window to open it, wanting to get a better view. She breathed in the rush of fresh, cherry–blossom–scented air. In disbelief of the scene outside, she leaned over and stuck out her head. Horses' hooves clattered as they pulled carriages and wagons. A cable car clanged as it made its ascent while an Oldsmobile motorcar tooted its horn as it sputtered by. Women in shirtwaist blouses and ankle–length skirts lifted their hems crossing the street while men attired in three–button suits with high–collared shirts, and bowler hats scurried about with canes and valises. Iron fences protecting flower gardens, blossoming trees, and grassy yards fronted pristine Victorian homes and row houses. Faith recognized some of the buildings but it was as if they had been stripped of their grime and age. From the blooming rhododendrons and daffodils she knew that it was still spring, but of the year she wasn't certain.

The door to her bedroom opened and Bridget walked in. She stepped back in startled surprise when she noticed Faith seated at the open window. Placing her hands on her broad hips, she seemed ready to scold as she approached.

"Too fine a day to be indoors, isn't it, with the sun shining and all those flowers blooming?" Bridget asked. "Made you chance fate and get out of bed, didn't it?"

"I just wanted some light and fresh air but I think I got more than I bargained for."

"The walk wore you out, didn't it? Just because you're feeling better doesn't mean you're cured."

Faith turned to face the maid and asked in a serious tone, "What's the date today?"

"April 8."

"What year?"

Bridget tilted her head. "The year? 1906."

"1906?" Faith swallowed hard.

"Yes, ma'am."

"Could you get me a newspaper?"

"Of course, ma'am." Bridget curtsied, pivoted and rushed out of the room.

She returned a few minutes later holding the *Chronicle*. She handed the newspaper to Faith who snatched it from her.

"Quite a pity what happened in Italy with the volcano erupting and all. So many poor souls killed," Bridget commented with a sigh.

Faith gaped at the headline that announced, in bold letters, the tragic eruption of Mount Vesuvius. The news jolted her into the realization that this episode wasn't a sick joke. Somehow, she had transcended the bounds of time and had ended up back in another era. *How?*

She tried to act composed when the unsettling fear of being trapped back in time overcame her. She felt like an alien who had just landed on another planet, an outcast. This wasn't her world.

She was a woman who had thrived on material possessions and on the luxuries of modern convenience. How could she cope in a turn–of–the–century lifestyle? What about her family and her friends? None of them were even born yet! What about her job? She was a teacher but her tools were the calculator and computer. If it was indeed 1906 she would be alone, a stranger. 1906.

Suddenly, she remembered the earthquake. San Francisco was devastated by a major earthquake and fire in 1906. Wasn't it on April 18? What was the date? April 8.

Overwhelmed over things that were out of her control, Faith began to panic. Beads of sweat formed and began to roll down her forehead. Her limbs trembled. As her heart quickened its beat, she gasped for breath. She curled up in the chair, bringing her legs up against her chest, seeking protection, and grasped them with her arms in a reassuring hug.

Bridget ran toward her. Faith wouldn't move but softly moaned.

Bridget rushed out of the room seeking help.

Doctor Forrester dashed into the room and to Faith's side. Putting one arm around her, he used the other to lift her up and out of the chair. He held her tight in his arms as he carried her to the bed. Tears rolled from her eyes as she mumbled incoherently. As if tucking in a child, Dr. Forrester laid her on the bed and covered her with the sheets and quilt.

"Bridget, fetch me a basin of cool water and a rag. Make haste!" he barked.

Bridget scurried out of the room.

Faith gazed up at the doctor as he leaned down to examine her. He was so close she could feel the warmth of his minty breath and spicy masculine scent. She looked up at him. His was an arresting face with a strong bone structure, a solid square jaw, and high cheekbones. Black lashes, unusually long and wispy for a man, framed dark almond eyes. His bushy black brows and wavy black hair added to his dramatic appearance.

Withdrawing a stethoscope from his suit pocket, he put on the headset and ear tips and placed the chest piece on her chest. His gentle fingers slid the cool chest piece over the flannel night-gown. His touch, so close to her flesh, made her flinch and tingle.

"What is it that upset you so?" he asked, removing the stethoscope and putting it back in his pocket.

"You…you wouldn't understand," she mumbled.

"There's a great deal that I don't understand about you. Perhaps, it's about time you start explaining. A doctor cannot help a patient about whom he knows so little."

Faith quietly watched him as he stood and went to retrieve a nearby chair. He placed the wicker chair at her bedside and sank his tall, lanky body in it.

Bridget returned with a small metal basin of water and a cotton rag. The doctor took them from her and placed the basin on the bed. He swished the rag in the water and rang it out.

"Thank you, Bridget. You may attend to your other duties now."

"Yes, sir." Bridget curtsied and left.

The doctor placed the damp cloth on Faith's forehead. She quivered as the cold touched her warm skin.

"Now, tell me. How did you end up on the bank near Golden Gate Park wet, strangely attired, and near death? Where did you come from?" he asked, eyes boring into her for answers.

"If I told you, you wouldn't believe me. You'd really write me off as being crazy."

"Perhaps." He removed the cloth from her head and returned it to the basin.

She sighed. "I wish I knew how I ended up here, in this place and time, and why. It doesn't make sense."

"You say, place and time? Bridget said that you became hysterical when she told you the date and handed you today's newspaper. Why?" he asked, his eyes darkening with the intensity of his gaze.

"As I said, you wouldn't understand. Just like you didn't understand Tylenol and couldn't understand cellular phone."

He shrugged. "I still don't. Perhaps, if you explain it will help."

He rang out the cloth and placed it on her forehead again.

"How can I explain that in the year 2006 I accidentally drove my car over a cliff into San Francisco Bay, only to be found on its banks in 1906?" she asked, beginning to tremble at the thought.

He knit his brows and glared at her.

She met his gaze. "I warned you wouldn't believe me."

"It's preposterous. You're asking me to believe that you have gone back in time one hundred years?"

"Yes. I don't know how or why."

He scoffed in agitation. "I've heard that gypsies can be beguiling but you, Madame, have mastered the art."

"You think I'm a gypsy?"

"Only gypsies weave strange tales, wear indecent garments, wear numerous earbobs, claim no past, and predict the future."

She had the urge to laugh at his ranting and raving and his thinking that she was a gypsy because she was from the future. This wasn't a laughing matter, though. She was as confused as he was about the turn of events. How can one explain that which defies explanation?

"Is that what you really think?"

"What else am I to think? That you dropped out of the sky from one hundred years hence? What nonsense!" He pulled the cloth off her forehead and threw it in the basin, causing a splash.

"You're a doctor, a scientific man. I should think if anyone could understand my plight it would be you."

He stood. "Don't toy with me. As soon as you are well enough, you can reunite with your clan on the Barbary Coast. You can go cast your spells on some unsuspecting oaf!"

He abruptly turned and marched out of the room.

She lay in bed wondering what was to become of her.

CHAPTER 2

FAITH GAZED IN THE OVAL hand mirror that Bridget had lent her. The haunting reflection made her gasp. Gone was her perfectly chiseled face, replaced by sunken cheeks, angular bones, and hollow eyes. Her glowing ivory complexion had turned pasty and sallow. Her eyebrows needed tweezing and dark roots were growing out from the center part of her hair. "California blonde" was returning to mousy brunette. In disgust she threw the mirror at her side on the bed, closed her eyes and settled back against the pillows. No wonder Doctor Forrester had been avoiding her.

A gentle knock rapped on her door.

"Come in," Faith said, opening her eyes.

Bridget ambled in with a silver tray laden with a tea set, scones, and teacakes. She set down the tray on the bedside table with a rattle and turned to Faith.

"Tea time, ma'am. Some sweets to put some meat on your bones."

"Don't drill it in, Bridget." Faith sighed. "I know how dreadful I look."

"Nothing that some food and time can't heal."

"And some Clairol."

"What ma'am?" Bridget tilted her head, stray strands of carrot red hair escaping from her starched, frilled cap.

"Oh, you wouldn't understand. I just took so much for granted: peroxide, hair coloring, makeup, manicures," Faith said, inspecting her ragged nails and chipped red polish.

Bridget shook her head, her gaze puzzled.

"I just want to return to normal."

"Ma'am, if your appearance is bothering you, perhaps I can be of some assistance. Before coming to work for the good doctor, I had been a lady's maid. I can help you with your toilette," Bridget said, beaming with self–assurance.

"I would be a challenge."

"It would be my pleasure." Bridget smiled, her apple cheeks glowing.

"Looking good is akin to feeling good."

Faith met her gaze. "You have been so kind to me. I'll put myself in your hands."

"After you've had your tea I'll return with my bag and I'll see what I can do."

Later, Bridget returned and eased Faith into a wicker chair. She opened her satchel of grooming aids. Faith watched in fascination as Bridget withdrew items from the bag like a magician revealing props. These props, though, were grooming aids from another era. The five–prong waving iron, a braided wire hair roll, a tortoise-shell pompadour comb, and boar bristle brush were considered antiques to Faith.

"It's been so long since I've worked for a lady," Bridget said, picking up the hairbrush, she stepped behind Faith and began to brush her thick and tangled mane in caressing strokes. The effect was soothing and was the first grooming Faith had had since entering this bewildering time and place.

"You work magic with that brush."

"That's quite a compliment, ma'am, coming from a gypsy and all."

"Do you really believe I'm a gypsy?"

"I don't know otherwise. I've always been quite fascinated with gypsies."

"Sorry to disappoint you but, contrary to what Doctor Forrester believes, I am not a gypsy. I'm a schoolteacher."

"Ma'am, it isn't my place to question but…" Bridget hesitated.

"Go on."

"I was wondering. Where did you come from?"

"If I told you the truth you'd think me insane. Let me say that I come from a strange place far away that longer exists. I am a refugee without a home or family."

She choked on her words, feeling as lost and alone as an astronaut on Mars. The worst part was, she didn't know how or why. Bridget stopped brushing and stood for a moment in contemplative silence.

"Bridget, I'm sorry I can't answer your question more thoroughly now. In time you'll learn the truth," she said, glancing back at the maid.

Bridget took a step back.

"Please, trust me rather than fear me. I really want to be your friend. God knows, I need a friend." Faith met Bridget's confused gaze.

"Oh." Bridget sighed as if a load had been taken off her back. "Why should I fear you? I, too, am a refugee. Left my homeland in Ireland. Left my family and all my friends to begin a new life here."

"So you can understand my plight?"

She nodded. "Yes, ma'am."

While Bridget continued to brush her hair, Faith tried to contemplate her future. Wasn't it ironic that she would be starting a new life in a different place and time? Rather, same place, different time. If she was back in her modern world she would also be starting over. Either way, hers would be a new life without Brad. Just thinking about Brad made her seethe. This entire predicament was his fault.

"Ouch," Faith squealed as her hair was yanked.

"Sorry, ma'am, just a nasty tangle."

Faith glanced back at Bridget and smiled. She really did need a friend. She needed someone to help her adjust to life in this old new world. Bridget, who seemed so trusting and caring, could teach her. After all, she had come over from Ireland and had learned to survive. One thing Faith knew was that she, herself, was a survivor.

"Now, isn't that better?" Bridget asked with a contented grin. She handed Faith the hand mirror and stepped back to admire her handiwork.

With hesitation, Faith accepted the mirror and peered into it. This time, the reflection shone more to her liking. The upswept pompadour hairstyle was quite elegant and refined. Faith had never worn her hair up before and was surprised at the Gibson Girl effect. Bridget had even done a commendable job of hiding the dark roots. She sighed. If she only had her foundation, blusher, mascara, and a dab of lipstick.

"Is something wrong, ma'am?" Bridget asked.

"You're a genius at hair styling. If I just wasn't so pale."

"But a lily–white complexion is a sign of beauty."

Faith shook her head, setting down the mirror. There was so much to get used to.

"Bridget, my hair is lovely but I can't go about in a nightgown. Could you bring me my clothes?"

"You mean the things you were wearing when the good doctor found you?" She frowned.

"Yes, my clothes."

"Ma'am, you can't be seen out and about in those."

"And why not?"

Bridget made a clucking sound with her tongue, turned on her heels, and walked over to the dresser. Out of a drawer she removed Faith's clothes. She waved the tan leather mini skirt.

"Your clothes have shrunk. This is most indecent." She tossed the mini skirt on the bed.

She picked up the silk ribbed turtleneck. "This is unacceptable."

She threw the sweater on the bed and retrieved the nude pantyhose, a thong bikini, and a lacy Wonderbra. "And these. I don't know what they are but they seem like something a proper lady wouldn't be caught dead wearing!"

Faith covered her mouth with her hand and laughed. Bridget stood before her, hand on her hips like a den mother with a stern gaze and an attitude to match.

Faith continued to laugh. The whole scene seemed too preposterous to be true. After the laughter came tears. She looked at each article of clothing and grasped them to her chest, one by one. They were all she had, the only reminders of her previous life, a life that was her past, and, seemingly, not her future.

"Ma'am?" Bridget glanced down and smoothed her apron. "I'm sorry if I've upset you."

Faith sniffled. "No. You were just being honest. You're right. I can't wear these things. It's 1906, isn't it?"

Bridget nodded, looking up.

"What does the well-dressed woman of 1906 wear?"

"You really don't know?"

"Not exactly. Can you help me?"

"I can go up to my quarters and see what I can do. This past year I've gained a wee bit of weight and some of my clothes just don't fit. Perhaps they can be altered for you."

"Oh, Bridget, you are a saint. Please go check."

The cotton shirtwaist was a little big but Faith's padded bra did fill it out and the white blouse did tuck neatly into the gray Melton cloth skirt. Even without a corset, the skirt fit well, a credit to Bridget's skill with a needle and thread. Over Bridget's objections, Faith donned her pantyhose and slipped her feet into a worn pair of Bridget's black oxfords. Though a little snug, they did complement the somber outfit. She just wished that she hadn't lost her kidskin pumps in the bay during the accident.

Faith stood, and with Bridget's assistance, paced her bedroom. At least her strength had returned and she was able to walk, albeit slowly. There was so much to learn and re–learn. When she approached the rosewood wardrobe, she stopped to inspect her appearance in the full–length beveled mirror. She looked like a dowdy nun even though Bridget assured her she was in fashion. Though she was fully attired, something was missing. As she touched her forefinger to her earlobe she remembered.

"Bridget, what happened to the jewelry I was wearing when I came here?" She hoped that they hadn't been stolen prior to her arrival. The way things were going, anything seemed possible.

"The jewelry, ma'am?"

"Yes, my earrings, necklace, wristwatch, bracelet, and ring?"

"Oh. Doctor Forrester put them away for safe keeping."

"He did, did he? Now that I'm feeling better I would like them returned."

"You will have to ask the doctor."

Faith pivoted to face her. "Let's go and ask him. He is home? I heard voices in the house."

"He's entertaining in the front parlor. It may not be wise to disturb him."

"Considering the fact that he's rarely home, I think it's as good a time as any." Faith hobbled toward the open door and stepped out into the upstairs hall. For a moment she stood still, surveying the flocked wall covering, glimmering stained–glass window and transom on the landing, and the handrails and banisters of the mahogany staircase. Everything was almost the same as when it was her home in 2006. Even the wall covering had a similar neutral pattern and beige hue. The familiarity of the surroundings made her shiver. She hugged herself.

"When I descend the staircase, the front parlor is on the left. The fireplace mantel is carved marble, a French antique," Faith murmured, remembering.

"How do you know?" Bridget asked. "You've never been downstairs and I've never told you."

"I just know," Faith replied, beginning her descent down the steep stairs, grasping the handrails for support and calculating her every step. As she looked down, she noticed that even the Persian runner was similar in design to the one she had purchased and placed.

Bridget hovered close behind.

"This isn't a good idea," Bridget whispered.

"It's my idea. What are you afraid of?"

Upon reaching the newel post, she stepped into the foyer. The parquet floor was as shiny and buffed as she had kept it. A complementing Persian scatter rug was placed in the exact same spot where she had hers. She drew a deep breath. Even the scent of freshly cut flowers wafted from a vase set on a hall table just as she would have in her home. Wasn't this her home, too?

She turned and glided into the parlor with an air of confidence.

Doctor Forrester's dark eyes met hers. Under slanted brows they glared like the burning embers in the hearth that he stood adjacent to. A woman's back was facing the door. Her petite hourglass figure was silhouetted in front of the doctor's dark, towering form. Both were formally attired in fine silk, he in a black tuxedo, and she in a navy ball gown.

"What is it, Doctor?" the woman asked in a girlish whine, turning to face the doorway and the subject of his rapt attention.

She was an attractive young creature. Strawberry blonde hair was pouffed up in a pompadour in front and taken up at the back to a chignon on top of her small head. Three pale pink feathers decorated her hair. Her features were delicate, set in a classically oval face. Her complexion was flawless, unblemished by age or the elements. Her pale green eyes, though, had a fire in them, revealing a girl who was used to getting her way. Young and spoiled, Faith thought. She also thought that the navy gown was a bit harsh, even with its pale pink cummerbund and underskirt, for such a young woman.

Faith looked away from the girl and focused her attention on the doctor, who looked a little too old to be with such a young woman and seemed agitated to have his liaison interrupted. Even men in this era are after young stuff, Faith thought.

"I wish to speak to the doctor," Faith requested, trying to ignore his icy stare, feeling as if she were being x–rayed.

"Who are you?" the young woman asked, and turning to the doctor, fluttering her spidery eyelashes, "Who is she? A patient you keep locked away in the attic?"

"She—"

"Miss Donahue is the new governess," Bridget chimed in, entering the room from the foyer.

"What?" Faith choked on the word.

Bridget came to her side and nudged her with an elbow in the ribs.

"Yes, Miss Donahue is…is…the new governess. That's who she…is," the doctor stammered.

"But, darling, I thought it was decided I would be choosing Andrew's new governess. I am, after all, your betrothed and soon to be Andrew's new mother."

The young woman pouted, gazing up demurely at the doctor.

"I know, Constance, but…but Andrew needed someone now. With all the poor lad's gone through you can surely understand?" the doctor assured with a forced smile.

"I can try."

"Excuse me," Faith interrupted. "Doctor, we have some matters to discuss."

"Yes, of course. Perhaps in the morning would be a better time," he answered, beads of perspiration forming above his brow.

"In the morning," Faith agreed with an exaggerated pout, a direct imitation of

Constance, that did not go unnoticed by the doctor.

Once in her room, Faith sat on her bed and let out a heavy sigh. Her gaze burned at Bridget who stood at the foot of the bed.

"Now, now. Don't you be getting angry at me, ma'am," Bridget said.

"I thought you were my friend."

"A better friend than you realize."

"By telling lies?"

"Maybe. Maybe not."

"What are you saying?"

"Constance LaDue is a little trollop all set to entrap the good doctor. She's all beauty and no brains. Being no more than a child herself, she's going to need help in caring for Andrew."

"Who is this Andrew?"

"The doctor's son."

"He was married?" Faith sat up erect, eager to hear more.

"Oh, yes. So very sad." Bridget came to Faith's side, plopping on the bed next to her. "He built this house for his wife only to have her die before it was finished. Died after childbirth, a frail young miss with a heart of gold. Ten times the girl than this
    Constance," Bridget explained with a curl in her lip and a snarl in her voice.

"How long ago did she die?"

"Four years to the month."

"I see, so Andrew is four? Doesn't he have a governess?"

"Had one. Miss Martin married and left to govern her own brood. So now you see, little Andrew needs a governess. You, ma'am, will be needing a profession now that you're well. You're intelligent and said that you were a schoolteacher. Besides, this house gets awfully gloomy and I could use a friend."

Faith met her gaze. "And Constance?"

"Ha! All she needs is a mirror."

They laughed like teenagers exchanging school gossip.

"What makes you so certain that the doctor will hire me? After all, he thinks I'm a gypsy."

"Tell him the truth, about your being a teacher and all. Here's your chance to prove it."

"Bridget, why are you so kind to me?"

"I don't know, but it's been said that every good deed is re-turned ten–fold."

CHAPTER 3

FAITH SLOUCHED IN THE VELOUR tapestry upholstered sofa. The fire in the hearth had burned down from the night before, the scorched embers scenting the parlor like acrid incense. She glanced about the room noticing the difference from how she had decorated it decades later. In place of her cream Berber, floral carpeting covered the floor.

Embossed stripes papered walls that she had painted white.

Heavy Baghdad draperies with cords and tassels accented the long narrow windows on which she had vertical blinds. The carved mantel of Carrera marble, that had always seemed so out of place in her contemporary surroundings, belonged in this room. She remembered how she had to argue with Brad to keep the mantel. He had wanted to replace it with vented glass. The mantel belonged in the room just as she felt she belonged. A chill tingled up her arms, to her shoulders and neck.

The pocket doors slid open and in marched Doctor Forrester. Attired in a striped wool suit, the double–breasted jacket accented his trim form, but the high–fastening collar was crisp, proper, and all business.

Seething through clenched teeth, he said, "I don't know what game you're playing but my son will not be a part of it."

She sat up in erect attention. "I don't know what you mean."

"About last night."

"Doctor, it seems to me that you were saved from a rather embarrassing situation. Surely, your intended would not think well of a man who treats female patients alone in his home."

"I haven't hired you on as governess." He stood looking down at her.

"Though it wouldn't be a bad idea," she replied, standing to face him. She refused to be intimidated by his close stance and serious demeanor. "I am, after all, a teacher by training and experience."

"Surely amongst the gypsies," he scoffed.

"That's your belief but not the truth. You did say that your son needs a governess now. Perhaps I can be of help on a trial basis. If you or your betrothed are not satisfied with my services, you can terminate my employment. If I prove to be successful, a long–term contract can be negotiated."

He shoved his hands in his pants pockets. "I don't know you. I don't know where you come from or what qualifications and references you hold."

"Though my references, transcripts, and paperwork are un-available at present, you must trust that I have taught elementary and middle grades for the past ten years. In college I had a double major in education and in history."

"In college?" He withdrew his right hand and stroked his chin.

She nodded.

"Still, my son is the most important person in my life. I won't entrust his care and education to just anyone."

"Doctor, no matter who you hire, she will be a stranger to you and to your son."

He sighed, putting his hand down at his side. "Is this what you came to ask me when you barged in last night?"

"No."

"No?" His brows arched and eyes tightened to narrow slits.

He seemed to be squinting to get a better look and under-standing of her. Faith drew a deep breath and straightened up to her full height, up to his shoulders. She wanted him to know that she wasn't some tiny and helpless little woman.

"I came downstairs to inquire about my belongings. My jewelry is missing and Bridget assured me that you're holding my things for safekeeping."

"Your jewelry?"

"My things are very important to me. I have very little in this world and what I do have is of great value to me. I just want returned what belongs to me."

He snickered. "How do I know that some poor soul hasn't lost these gems to your sticky fingers?"

"I shouldn't be accused of stealing what is rightfully mine."

"Very well." He turned and motioned for her to follow. "Come with me."

She smoothed her skirt and followed the doctor across the foyer and into the dining room. She was impressed with the brass chandelier with its frosted glass globes, the carved pillar dining table, cane seat chairs, and elaborately carved and ornamented sideboard. It was a far cry from the glass and chrome dining room set Brad had chosen for their room.

Set in one corner was a boxy object that resembled an end table with its faux wood grain finish, molded cast iron legs, and veined marble top. The doctor knelt down before its door, touched a button to drop the decorative metal cover, revealing a combination lock dial and brass handle.

"Oh, it's a safe," Faith said.

"Yes." The doctor looked up at her over his shoulder. "My parlor safe for heirlooms and other things I value. Do you mind turning around while I work the combination?"

"How dare you consider me a risk?"

"Madame, I hardly know you to consider you otherwise."

"Are you always so trusting of people?"

"Turn around," he ordered, motioning with his hands.

With a huff she obeyed, turning to face the wall. She could hear the dial squeaking as he manipulated the lock. With a click and a clunk of the locking bolts disengaging, she could tell that he opened the safe.

"Can I turn around now or are you afraid I might see what's

inside?" she asked.

"Wait," he replied, shuffling through the safe. After, he closed the door and spun the dial.

"Here are your things," he said, standing.

She turned to face him. In his broad palms he held her engagement-wedding rings, diamond ear studs, heavy gold loop earrings, diamond solitaire pendant, gold bangle bracelet, and her Movado museum wristwatch.

"Great," she said, visually inspecting her belongings, feeling a bit melancholy at seeing the only reminders of her past, except for the ring that reminded her of Brad.

"Where would someone like you get such diamonds and gold? Theft or gifts from …er…admirers?"

"I bought most of them myself," she said, casting him an icy stare for what he had implied.

She removed the pieces of jewelry, one by one, from his hands and put them on.

He watched in amusement as she donned the multiple earrings and bracelet. The watch's style seemed to confound him and the rings confuse him. As she struggled to clasp the necklace, he drew his hands up to her neck and grabbed the clasp.

"Let me," he offered.

Before she could refuse, his warm hands brushed the back of her neck, searing her flesh. Tingles prickled as delicate hairs stood on end at his touch. She gasped at the unexpected electric feelings he caused.

"All set," he said with a satisfied grin dimpling his cheeks.

She turned away feeling the color rise in her cheeks. She hadn't blushed since she was a teenager. This didn't make sense.

"The jewelry is lovely, I must admit, but is quite unusual." He stood analyzing her. "The earbobs seem like something found in an African tribe and I have never seen such a timepiece."

"Oh," she said, glancing at her wristwatch and realizing how out of place it must be in an era of pocket watches with chains.

"I don't know if I will ever understand you Miss or is it Missus

Donahue?" His eyes were drawn to the engagement–wedding rings on her left hand.

"Papa, papa!" a little boy screamed, scurrying into the dining room, dragging a ratty blue blanket. With his slick black hair, ebony eyes, and strong bones, he was a miniature version of his father. Except for the knee pants, even the striped wool suit resembled his father's.

Doctor Forrester's eyes sparkled as he stooped down to gather the little bundle of energy into his arms. He hugged the child in an intimate embrace. The love generated between father and son made Faith feel like an intruder in their midst.

The little boy's eyes met hers. She smiled in response, feeling a tug at her heart.

Pointing a finger at her, the child asked, "Is that my new mommy?"

Doctor Forrester met her startled gaze. "No, son, Miss Donahue is your new governess."

"Oh, goody!" the boy screeched, squirming out of his father's grasp.

Faith reacted quickly and bent down to catch the child as he jumped into her arms. She squeezed him gently as he nuzzled against her chest, his little arms clinging around her neck. She caressed his silky hair and looked down into his plump cherub face. He was an enchanting child.

"The boy is spoiled. I fear I've bestowed too much love on the child since his mother died," the doctor said with a lump in his throat.

"One can never give a child too much love. Considering the circumstances, it's understandable," Faith said, hugging the little boy and gazing up at his father.

"He needs discipline. The last governess tried to turn him into a sissy."

"Has he had many governesses?"

"Only one. Andrew had grown quite attached to her, like to a mother. She married and left my employ. The boy was devastated. This time things will be different. Andrew will have both a mother and a governess. When Constance and I marry, he will finally have the mother he needs for love and a governess, Miss Donahue, to educate him. It is an arrangement that should stabilize our lives."

Or complicate them, Faith thought to herself.

CHAPTER 4

ANDREW FORRESTER WAS A FOUR-YEAR old keg of dynamite. Faith was at wits end keeping up with his rambunctious energy and inquisitive curiosity. Out of all the children she had dealt with through the years, Andrew was the most challenging.

He had a blatant disregard for authority. Discipline was just another game. He desperately needed spanking but when he looked up at her through his dark lashes, his dimpled smile radiating from his angelic face, she could do nothing but forgive his indiscretions. Faith knew that she was putty in his manipulative little hands.

Faith allowed Andrew the freedom of choosing his own games, stories, and activities. Anything to stop him from screaming, and having tantrums that echoed throughout the house. She had to keep the peace to keep her position, as tenuous as it was. This was all she had in this strange new world and there was no telling if she'd ever return to the old one.

Faith just wished there were a television for Sesame Street or Barney, or a VCR for Disney videos, or a computer to keep his brain and little fingers out of trouble. She realized that parenting in the early part of the century was actively hands-on. There were fairy tales to be read, a primer to study numbers and the alphabet, building blocks, mechanical toys, and a slingshot she had to hide more than once.

After playing a game of hide-and-seek in the garden, Faith decided it was far too sunny and warm to stay in their yard. She had thought of venturing out and away from the house many times but an alarm at the unknown kept her from acting. The city away from the safety of 92 Sacramento Street seemed more intimidating than a visit to a foreign country. She realized that if circumstances had brought her to this point in time, she had no choice but to adapt. So far, she thought, she had been adapting quite well.

Faith pulled Andrew's shiny steel express wagon to the front walk. Andrew, trailing behind, eagerly jumped in and sat holding his blankie and favorite stuffed bear.

During moments like these, when he was all cute and innocent, she just stared at him feeling sorry for them both. Thoughts of their losses would drift through her mind. He lost his mother and she lost a marriage and hopes of motherhood.

She grasped the wagon's handle and pulled, walking down the street and back in time. Stately Victorian mansions in the arched Italianate, gabled Queen Ann styles, and brick and painted row houses lined Sacramento Street. There were no glass curtainwall highrises to dwarf the fine homes or obstruct the view of the bay. Everything was pristine and new. As she inhaled, even the air had a fresh scent. There was no car or bus exhaust, only a faint scent of manure mingled with cherry blossoms.

She also noticed the quiet. Yes, there was the rattle of carriages and the jingle of harness bells, an occasional putt–putt of an automobile or a clanging cable car, but there were no irate drivers blasting horns, car brakes squealing, or emergency sirens blaring. There was peace and calm.

As she walked she felt more like a guest on vacation than a resident of Pacific Heights. In a way she was, going back 100 years. She wondered if their destination had existed in 1906.

Lafayette Park had been her oasis from the concrete jungle that San Francisco had been in 2006. She smiled as they approached the familiar four–block square of community park. Gone were the joggers and Frisbee–dog teams. In their place were governesses pushing babies in netted perambulators or picnicking with their charges.

She appeared a little out of place. The other governesses were attired in crisp, starched uniforms with matching hats and long gloves. They cast her a frigid glare. She felt naked and, in their eyes, was probably as close to naked as a woman could become in public. Without a hat, elbow–length gloves, and dark stockings, she did look out of place. Why hadn't Bridget or the doctor warned her about her appearance? Wasn't the doctor ashamed to have her watching over his son? Maybe he just wanted her to fail as a governess. She began to get knots in her stomach.

As she looked around at the lush green grass and sturdy trees, an eerie fear crept up in her stomach, making her nauseous. The date was April 12. In six days this tranquil city would be destroyed and forever changed by a devastating earthquake and fire.

"What's wrong, Miss Donahue?" Andrew asked, peering up from the wagon.

She turned to meet his wide–eyed gaze. "Nothing's wrong, Andrew. Everything will be just fine."

From that moment on, she assured herself, everything would be fine. She'd see to it. They would get through one of the greatest American catastrophes unscathed.

She reached down and lifted Andrew out of the wagon. He grasped his blankie and bear securely in his dimpled hands. He sat on the grass and she knelt down to face him.

"Let's play in the park this morning and enjoy this lovely weather and the calm while we still can."

After the excursion to the park and time for cleaning up, Faith joined Andrew in the dining room for lunch. The oval dining table was covered in pastel coral linen and set with sparkling china, sterling, and crystal. Faith set the boy in a booster seat and sat next to him. Bridget entered from the butler's pantry with a pitcher of freshly squeezed lemonade that she poured into their glasses. As she walked out of the dining room, Doctor Forrester stepped in.

"Miss Donahue," he said, standing by his chair at the head of the table. "From now on I must ask you take your meals in the servant's quarters. I also had Bridget move your things up to an appropriate room. It is only proper that those in my employ reside and dine in their appropriate quarters."

He pulled out his chair, sat, and fanned his linen napkin on his lap.

"And what of Master Andrew and his learning of proper etiquette?" Faith asked.

"Miss LaDue will be handling that task after we are married."

"I hate her!" Andrew squealed.

"Who?" the doctor asked, staring at Faith.

"Miss LaDue! Yuck!" Andrew banged his tiny fist on the table and scrunched up his face.

"You mustn't say such things. Miss LaDue is to be your mother," Doctor Forrester said, glancing at his son and Faith, "Apparently your teaching the boy proper etiquette isn't effective."

Faith held her tongue, rose from her seat, and stepped away from the table, throwing down her napkin.

"You will have to excuse me. I'm going to have lunch in the servant's quarters where I am welcome." She scurried to the doorway, ignoring his intense gaze and satisfied grin.

"Miss Donahue," the doctor called.

She reluctantly stopped and swiveled to face him.

"I was informed that Andrew enjoyed his visit to Lafayette Park this morning. I've planned a picnic for supper. He and Miss LaDue are joining me in Golden

Gate Park to fly a new kite."

"I hope you have an enjoyable time," she said, turning away. She wanted to tell him where he could fly his kite but bit her tongue.

"Miss Donahue," he called again.

She turned, rolling her eyes.

"You are coming with us to supervise Andrew."

The wide expanse of lush green lawn was the perfect setting for a Saturday outing. A warm, gentle breeze kicking up from the bay made the diamond–shaped kite billow overhead streaming its tail of fabric bows. Andrew touched the string to which the kite was tethered. His eyes were transfixed on the multicolored kite as it climbed higher and higher riding on waves of air. Faith held the ball of string, releasing it through Andrew's fingers. She feared giving the whole ball to him, knowing that the pull of the kite was far too strong for his grasp. She also didn't want to lose the object of their entertainment.

She cast a glance at Doctor Forrester who stood poised like a military officer. His hands were knotted behind his back and a satisfied grin shone on his face as he watched his son giggle over the kite. She wondered what he was thinking while gazing at the miniature duplicate of himself. Perhaps, it was of his wife, the boy's mother. Or was it Constance LaDue, who stood at his side fidgeting from boredom.

Faith wondered what he saw in the girl. She was pretty but not breathtakingly beautiful. Her figure was fair even with the boosts a corset and bustle could provide.

Standing next to the doctor she looked small, like his child, not his betrothed. Faith wondered if she'd ever understand men.

"Oh, the wind is mussing my hair and the bugs, oh, they are so unbearable," Constance complained, swatting the air with her kidskin–gloved hands.

Faith stifled a laugh at hearing her. Constance hadn't stopped complaining since they arrived at Golden Gate Park. As a matter of fact, she complained as they motored on over. There was the dust, the speed, and the wind. The girl found a problem with everything and everyone. Faith was sure that she was also an object of the girl's scorn. Constance always arched her thin brows and huffed when their eyes met. She scrutinized Faith's disheveled appearance, shaking her head in disapproval.

Faith knew that she looked different but couldn't help it. Refugees, after all, were never known for their fashion sense or social savvy. If Constance didn't like her gold jewelry, bare hands, or nude hose, Faith didn't care. She knew that there was one thing Constance did like. Thanks to Faith, Andrew was kept away. The farther away Andrew was from Constance, the better. The girl lacked the patience and understanding necessary to deal with children, probably because she wasn't far from being a child herself.

"Oh, Doctor, how long must I stay out here? I shall get freckles," Constance said, gazing up at the doctor with her fluttering lashes over doe eyes.

"As long as Andrew wants. I promised him an afternoon frolic in the park and a picnic." He looked down at her with a grin. "Besides, my dear, with your netted hat, parasol, and long gloves, not one sun ray will touch your creamy soft skin."

Constance drew her hand up to her face to hide her blush.

"That kite has plenty of lift, son," the doctor yelled.

"Yes, papa! It wants to carry Miss Donahue away!" Andrew replied

"I wish it would," Constance muttered under her breath.

"What, dear?" the doctor asked.

"Lovely day," Constance said with a smirk.

Faith removed Andrew's fingers from the string and released more string from the ball, allowing the kite to soar higher. The kite, silhouetted against the blue sky, swayed in the air like a tethered bird fighting to be released. As she let go of more string, Faith ran across the lawn with Andrew in tow. They turned and ran, laughing aloud in joyful glee. Faith hadn't flown a kite since she was a child and it brought back distant memories.

"Shall we reel her in?" she asked Andrew, standing still.

"Yes! Oh, yes!" Andrew screamed, jumping up and down.

"Here we go." Faith began to wind in the string. The action took strength, the wind fighting her every step of the way. She pulled and pulled while Andrew cheered her on.

"Papa, papa! We're bringing her in!" Andrew yelled.

Doctor Forrester grasped Constance's arm and led her toward his son and Faith.

Faith struggled with the kite, trying to reel it in but knew that she was loosing the battle. She was no match for the powerful air currents. Her fingers were stinging from the string as it slid through them. With one jolt she felt the string snap. The quick release of tension sent her sprawling face down in the grass.

Andrew stood over her laughing and clapping his hands. When he saw his father approach, he pointed up to the sky where the kite was sailing away on a wave of ocean air.

"Well, she won her freedom," Faith said, sitting, smoothing her skirt, and regaining her composure.

Doctor Forrester offered her his hand. At first she was going to ignore his offer of assistance and get up on her own. She was an independent woman, wasn't she? One look at Constance's appalled expression made her change her mind. She was reminded of her status as a woman in 1906.

"Thank you, Doctor," Faith said as she accepted his firm grip in getting her back on her feet. His touch was so smooth and warm that for a moment she didn't want to let go.

"Are you all right?" he asked, still grasping her hand. His eyes were soft and sympathetic as they met hers.

"I'm fine…no broken bones…no harm done," she stammered, wavering. She wasn't sure if it was the fall or his gentle touch and gaze.

"Are you certain?" he asked.

"Yes, Doctor Forrester," she said, taking a deep breath.

He released her hand.

"Now that our kite is off on its own adventure, what do you say if we all have supper? Bridget, I've been told, has prepared a feast." Doctor Forrester took Andrew's hand and Constance's arm.

Faith stepped behind them as they strolled to the grassy knoll where the wicker picnic hamper was set on a checkered cloth.

Doctor Forrester removed the straw boater from his head and set it on the edge of the cloth. He went to the picnic hamper, unbuckled its leather straps, and lifted open the lid. He reached in and removed linen napkins that he handed to Constance, Andrew, and to Faith, who hesitated. She was still uncertain of her place.

"Miss Donahue, since you've proven yourself to be quite a kite–woman, won't you dine with us?" he asked, noting her discomfort.

"If no one objects," she replied, noting Constance's icy gaze.

"No one objects," he said, handing her the napkin.

She accepted it with caution.

"Are we going to sit on the ground like commoners?" Constance asked, standing while the doctor, Andrew, and Faith sat comfortably on the cloth.

"My dear, this is a picnic," the doctor said, patting a spot at his side.

"When we picnic at home it is with wrought iron chairs and tables in the garden."

"Constance, this is a park. Come now, don't be concerned. Look about. Others are doing the same," he assured.

She cast her gaze around the park and saw other groups of genteel people seated on blankets and tablecloths. Reluctantly, she eased herself down at his side. Ever so carefully she smoothed her skirt and assumed a discreet and proper pose, making sure to cover her ankles and to sit erect.

Faith stared at the girl wondering if this was the way a proper woman of the era would act or if Constance was the exception. Faith, in turn, adjusted her own body to appear more feminine. She had been lounging a bit, forgetting the time and place.

After a hearty supper of cold chicken, salad, muffins, bread, cheese, soda pop, and decadent chocolate cake, the doctor suggested a stroll. At first, Faith suggested that he and Constance go while she stayed behind and occupied Andrew. The doctor, though, insisted that they tag along.

Faith realized how much had changed in 100 years. Golden Gate Park had been just a park. The Golden Gate Bridge, its most noteworthy attraction, had yet to be constructed. Many museums had yet to be built, recreation areas planned, the famous carousel created, and paths set.

Faith reveled in the beauty of the Conservatory of Flowers as they walked amidst the tropical foliage, ferns, and scented orchids. She always admired the ornate wood–frame building and had been saddened when it was severely damaged in the storm of 1995. Many had thought it was beyond repair. To see it in its newly built splendor was almost worth the trip back in time. The expansive greenhouse and its blooming exhibits awed her. For a moment she closed her eyes to draw in the sweet, humid air.

A shriek up ahead disturbed her peace. She opened her eyes to see Constance flailing her arms and jumping around as if she had seen a mouse. As Faith approached, she noticed Andrew cowering behind a green palm frond. His slingshot, armed with a dried pea, was aimed at Constance's backside. A contented grin shone on his face as he aimed and fired.

Constance jumped, screaming in a near tantrum. She twirled around, touching her backside with her hands as if expecting to find serious damage. The doctor stood at her side trying his best to calm her "ants–in–her–pants" hysterics.

His eye caught Faith's as she grabbed Andrew in surprise, the slingshot dangling from his hand. She covered the boy's mouth with her hand to suppress his protests. As she set him down, she took his slingshot and hid it in her skirt pocket. The doctor let out a sigh, as if relieved over her quick actions.

Constance, who was too worried about herself to see Andrew's indiscretion, was so flustered she begged to be taken home at once.

That evening, after tucking Andrew into bed, Faith was met by the doctor in the dimly lit upstairs hallway.

"Is David asleep?" he asked, startling her.

"David?"

"Of Goliath fame." The doctor chuckled.

"Oh, yes," she said, smiling. "He's sound asleep."

She felt in her pocket and removed the slingshot. She handed it over to the doctor.

"He's quite a handful, isn't he?" he asked, brushing her hand as he took the slingshot. He inspected the weapon. "Like father, like son."

"Sir?"

"I wanted to tell you what a fine job you're doing with Andrew. I haven't been the most cordial employer. I've had my reasons. I just wanted you to know that your trial is going very well. Andrew likes you, but more than that, he respects you."

"All those years of teaching haven't been wasted, after all."

"Would you join me for some tea? I would like to learn more about your teaching experience and education?" he invited, his voice a silken caress, as his eyes met hers.

She hesitated. She wished that it was that easy, to sit and discuss her life over tea. He would never believe her when she told him about her degrees from colleges that had yet to exist, of her experience in teaching inner-city children, of computers, of history yet to be made, and theories to be invented. Oh, how she longed to tell someone, but if she told him she would most certainly lose the only position she held and a place in the only home she had known.

"Thank you, sir, but I'm quite exhausted. It's been a busy day. Perhaps, another time."

"Another time," he said, nodding his head and walking away.

She watched in silence as he headed down the hall to the main stairs. She sighed. Another time.

CHAPTER 5

FAITH HESITATED IN THE THRESHOLD. The library was much more scholarly looking than she remembered. In her time, the cherry paneled room was used as a den for casual television viewing. In this era, before television was invented, it resembled an office. A rectangular hand–carved desk sat in one corner with a matching mahogany and leather swivel chair. Spread open upon the desktop was a ledger with a pen and a pair of wire–rimmed reading glasses. Nearby, the fireplace blazed hot with wood and coal, taking away the evening chill. Next to it was an overstuffed armchair for cozy reading and a table with a lit kerosene lamp and overhead, a gas chandelier added a mellow ambiance.

Standing by a bookcase that lined one wall, was Doctor Forrester. He held a well–worn leather–bound volume in one hand while he scanned the jammed case in search of another. Observing him, Faith thought that he resembled the bust of Julius Caesar that was perched on a top shelf. He stood still, shoulders straight, head erect with a most serious expression on his face. He belonged amongst the books, the aged paper, the leather, dark wood, and the pungent scent of the fire.

She almost turned away as to not disturb him. Bridget had told her that the doctor retreated to his library every evening after dinner and that it was the best time to discuss matters with him.

"After a man's been fed and watered, he's much more agreeable," Bridget had said.

Faith wondered if the doctor was ever agreeable. There was one way to find out. Taking a deep breath, she rapped on the partially open pocket door to get his attention.

He spun around to face her, startled at the interruption. His eyes were wide and intense as they met hers, his lips forming a grim line.

"Doctor Forrester, I wondered if I might have a word with you?" Faith asked, stepping into the room.

"Seeing that I have just lost my train of thought, you may as well speak and get it over with," he said with a bite in his voice, slapping the leather book against his thigh.

"I have a simple request," she said. "Since I am employed as Andrew's governess, on a trial basis, of course, I think it only fitting that you provide me with a proper uniform."

"Miss Donahue, I'm one step ahead of you. I've requested Miss LaDue to procure a uniform appropriate to your station. I can't have a member of my household being seen in public in ragtag clothing, bare limbs, and ...improper unmentionables," he stuttered and waved his arm at the last word.

Faith glared at him. All she needed was a uniform chosen by that tart, Miss LaDue. Knowing the girl, it would probably be ugly, matronly black, and unflattering.

Wearing her present clothing was bad enough. Bare limbs? Improper unmentionables? Why, then, was he mentioning them? How did he know what she was wearing underneath her clothes?

Seeing the fire erupt in her cheeks and the glow of her aquamarine eyes, Ian Forrester began to fidget and pace the floor like a trapped lion, trapped by his words.

"Miss Donahue, I am quite aware of your lack of fashion sense and propriety."

"My...what?" she screamed. "Doctor, I'd like you to know that where I come from I have a room–size closet filled with designer clothing. Calvin Klein, Donna Karan, Liz Claiborne… even a Versace evening gown! Since I can't go back, I'm stuck here with hand–me–downs and your generosity. I don't look this way by choice but out of necessity!"

He looked at her, suddenly remorseful and rotten. She didn't deserve his embarrassing comments and insults. She was doing the best she could with what little she had. He perused her. Her shirtwaist was clean and starched, her skirt pressed, and her shoes polished. If not for Constance's comments, he wouldn't have been aware of her lack of proper undergarments. As for her bare hands, he thought it made more sense than donning kidskin gloves in the heat of spring and summer, even if it was socially improper. He had to admit that the flesh–toned hose was much more flattering than the black wool hose women wore. The vision of her romping with the kite, skirt aflutter, legs exposed made him suddenly hot. He drew a deep breath. Where was his sense of propriety? What was wrong with him?

"I apologize if I've hurt your feelings, Miss Donahue." He swallowed hard. Standing across from him she looked so shattered and alone like a lost child. He shouldn't be scolding her. "I am not familiar with the dress designers you've mentioned but am certain if you had your wardrobe you wouldn't be making a request from me."

"Sir, I wouldn't be asking you for anything if I had a choice."

That night, Faith couldn't sleep. She tossed and turned feeling as if she were on a ship in a storm–tossed sea. Visions of the earth swaying filled her mind with scenes of buildings tumbling over, brick–by–brick. Frantic people rushed into the streets in stages of undress as the buildings crumbled around them. Screams of terror, of pain, of death pierced the silence of dawn. Horse's neighing, ruptured gas lines hissing, water mains spouting added to the panic. Orange–red flames erupted, enveloping everything and everyone in stifling acrid heat. Hell. It could only be hell.

She sprang up in her bed, clammy in a cold sweat, her heart palpitating in such a beat she could feel its rhythm. The room was pitch black. She thought she was lost in a deep abyss, in the hell she had envisioned. For a moment she wondered if she was still alive.

A trembling fear grabbed at her heart. She wanted to scream but covered her mouth with her hands. Feeling trapped and smothered, she had to escape. In the dark she felt for her robe, the one Bridget had lent her. Finding it, she slipped it on, tying the belt. She pawed her way to the door.

As she stepped out into the hall, a figure with a candlestick and flickering candle startled her.

"What in blazes happened?" Bridget asked, flashing the candlelight in Faith's face, distorted shadows dancing on the walls.

Faith shielded the glaring light with her hands until her eyes could adjust to light.

"Thank God it's only you," Faith gasped.

"Who else might it be?"

"I…I thought, for a moment, that I might be dead or…or sent back."

"Back where?" Bridget cocked her head.

Getting hold of her senses, Faith replied, "Oh, I've had horrible nightmares. I needed to get out of that stifling room."

"Come with me, down to the kitchen. I'll warm some milk. You look like you've had quite a fright."

Bridget grasped Faith's hand. Like holding on to a child, she led Faith down the backstairs and into the kitchen. Once in the room, Bridget set the candlestick down on the worktable. She pulled up a chair and pointed to Faith to sit. Faith slunk down into the oak–spindled chair, leaning forward, elbows on the table. She watched Bridget light a kerosene floor lamp, bend down to scuttle coal from the coal hod into the cast–iron stove, and use a poker to stir up the banked fire. It was a far cry from turning on a knob and having instant heat.

Bridget waddled over to the oak, double–door icebox. She pulled on a brass handle and opened one door, removing a bottle of milk. Setting the glass bottle on the worktable, she removed a steel saucepan from an overhead pot rack. She filled the saucepan with milk and returned the remainder to the icebox. After placing the saucepan on the stovetop, she pulled up a chair and plopped in it.

"Now, tell me about your nightmare," Bridget said.

Faith stared at her. "If I told you, told anyone, they'd think me insane."

"I must say, you are different, but not ready for bedlam yet." Bridget grinned.

"My nightmare is far too real. Something is going to happen in a few days that is too catastrophic to be believed. It is something over which I have no control. I can only keep those I have grown close to out of harm's way. To warn everyone in San Francisco would be fruitless. Even if everyone did listen, panic would set in. History would be altered forever. You see, this knowledge is haunting me, just tearing me apart," Faith explained in an emotionless monotone. She had to tell someone, to give some warning about the impending danger. As much as she tried to stash away her fears, reality was fast approaching. The visions served as a reminder, a wake–up call. She could no longer keep the knowledge to herself. She knew that she couldn't live with herself if she did.

"One thing good about nightmares is they don't come true," Bridget commented in her jovial tone.

Faith looked up, straight into her eyes. "Bridget, this one is going to come true."

"I must go check on the milk." Bridget rose from her seat to tend to the pot on the stove.

"I know that you don't believe me. Who would? It seems beyond the realm of reason, I know." Faith let out a sigh. "I didn't ask for this."

"Ask for what?" Doctor Forrester asked, his dusky voice echoing from the doorway.

Faith turned and gasped at the thought of him eavesdropping. Attired in an elegant silk paisley robe, his dark hair tousled, a growth of beard shadowing his face, he looked better than a man ought in the wee hours of the morning. Faith thought it unfortunate that the handsome men tended to need attitude adjustments. They also happened to be overly inquisitive and in the habit of being in the wrong place at the wrong time. She didn't want to explain her passage through time at the moment. She was tired, cranky, and unprepared to deal with him.

"Miss Donahue had quite a nightmare," Bridget chirped. "Some warm milk can settle her down."

The doctor scratched his head, shuffling into the room. "I had my own nightmare."

"Perhaps you'll be in need of some warm milk, too?" Bridget asked.

"Only if you put some cocoa in it," he replied, sitting in the chair Bridget had vacated. He glanced over at Faith, who was attired in an oversized flannel robe, her hair casually falling over her shoulders, and realized how inappropriate the situation was. A man didn't allow unattached women to see him in his bedclothes. Likewise, a modest woman would remove herself from his sight, blushing and feigning apologies. Faith did neither. She sat firm in her seat unfazed by his casual attire and hers.

"I'd like cocoa in mine, too," Faith added.

"So, Miss Donahue, what has kept you up all night? Or, maybe, I'm being too forward to ask," the doctor said, analyzing her. For the life of him he just couldn't figure her out.

Faith drew away from his too alert gaze. It was bad enough that he had to appear in the kitchen, but having him seated so close with those inquiring eyes made her tremble.

"She's been having nightmares about the mayhem that is to befall the city in a few days," Bridget said with a giggle.

"What mayhem?"

Faith squirmed in her seat. "On April 18 at 5 a.m. a major

earthquake will rock the city and, soon after, a raging fire will destroy it."

"That's a pretty specific nightmare. So, what time does God appear after this Armageddon?" the doctor asked with a chuckle.

"In a few days this will not be so funny."

Bridget placed mugs of hot chocolate in front of the doctor and Faith but neither seemed to notice.

"Miss Donahue has been blessed or cursed with the gift of prophecy," Bridget commented.

"Only the Irish would believe such nonsense." Doctor Forrester scoffed.

"Sir, as I recall, you once told me of your Scotch–Irish ancestry," Bridget said, hands on her hips.

The doctor scowled. He wrapped his hands around the steaming mug of cocoa and lifted it up to his lips for a sip, savoring the sweet scent and taste. As he set the mug back on the table, he stared at Faith.

"I think it best, Miss Donahue, that you keep your dreams and your nightmares to yourself."

"Even if they offer a warning that can keep you and your household out of danger?" She met his intense gaze and held it, determined not to let him intimidate her. "I wanted to keep my secret but would feel remiss if I didn't warn you of the earthquake. I assure you that in the early morning of April 18, this house will tremble and some walls will crack but it will be safe. A raging fire will engulf the city due to ruptured gas lines and the lack of water pressure. Dynamiting will prevent the fire from spreading through this neighborhood. Nob Hill will be sacrificed but this street will be saved."

"What nonsense!"

"Believe what you will, but if you cherish your son, your staff, and your life, stay in this house. If you stay here, you will be safe. I guarantee it."

"How?"

"History. In 2006, this home and this street are as intact as they are now. Local archives tell the story of how this neighborhood was spared."

He growled, "More nonsense about a hundred years hence."

"It isn't nonsense."

Faith could see the doubt wrinkling his brow and in the raging embers in his dark eyes. His pupils were like glowing lumps of coal aimed directly at her. She closed her own eyes to regain her composure. She knew that she hadn't a choice but to warn him. How could she survive if they would perish or be harmed in the calamity without her warning?

"How?" he demanded.

"All that concerns me is that you and those you care about know what to expect and can prepare accordingly. Because I'm a part of your household, I feel responsible for your well–being."

He scoffed. "You will not be a part of this household for long if you continue speaking of such nonsense. Talk of being from the future, of earthquakes, and fires. I have the mind to send you packing so you can go back to where you came from."

"I wish that were possible."

He rose from his chair, his eyes wide and aglow. "Miss Donahue, I think that April 18 will be your day of reckoning!"

CHAPTER 6

"I CAN'T BELIEVE I'M ACTUALLY LISTENING to you. If the good doctor knew what we were doing behind his back, he would send both of us on our way," Bridget said, removing delicate crystal glasses from the rosewood china closet while Faith wrapped them in newspaper and packed them in a wooden crate.

"The good doctor will be appreciative when he learns that his heirlooms have been saved from the destruction of the earthquake."

"If there is, indeed, an earthquake."

"Come on, Bridget, you can't be doubting me, too." Faith snatched a goblet out of Bridget's hand.

Bridget turned to face her. "When I'm out and about the city, I just find it hard to believe. The whole event seems so unlikely."

"Yet, you follow my ideas?"

"Mainly because there's something so different about you, some far–off unexplained wisdom. You don't seem like someone from this world."

Faith's eyes sparkled. "So you believe me when I say that I come from the future?"

"I don't know what to believe, really." Bridget sighed. "Just what you say and how you say it frightens me enough to want to believe."

"Thank you for having an open mind."

Bridget reached up to remove another goblet as Faith wrapped the one in her hand and knelt down to set it in the crate. She smiled. Someone believed in her. Someone had faith in Faith.

"Little Master Andrew is still asleep, isn't he?" Bridget asked, handing her a water tumbler.

"I hope so. He naps until two and then he'll be ready for a snack and play." Faith took the tumbler and began to wrap it.

"He's really grown fond of you and minds you better than he did his other nanny."

"He's still quite a handful."

"Like his father," Bridget muttered.

"And why is that?"

"Doctor Forrester sometimes lacks all reason."

Faith snickered, bending to pack the tumbler. "When?"

"When Miss Constance LaDue entered his life. She places so many demands on him and they are not yet married. I don't know how he'll be able to carry on the practice with her under foot. She's in constant need of attention."

"She's just a spoiled child who needs to grow up." Faith stood, placed her hands on her waist, and stretched.

"A man in his position needs a wife who is a responsible woman. Where is his common sense?"

"For men, sense is not common."

Bridget laughed. "Men don't marry for the right reasons, do they? They'd rather be chasing youth and beauty."

Faith smiled. Some things stayed the same through the centuries. She thought about Brad and his cute, young blonde. Funny, she had been so wrapped up in adjusting to her new life, she had pushed thoughts of him to the back of her mind. For the first time, she wondered if he missed her, if anyone missed her.

"You look worried, ma'am. You have no need to worry. You're young and pretty."

"Young and pretty? That's an opinion," Faith said. If she was so desirable, why did Brad dump her?

Bridget made clucking sounds with her tongue and said, "I'm thinking that you have been jilted by a suitor and that's why you left your home."

Faith froze in place.

"I'm right, am I not?" Bridget asked in a "told you so" tone.

"Partly. My husband left me for a much younger woman. I didn't leave my home by choice, though. Coming here was some sort of fluke accident."

"Ah, you left home by fate."

"Yes…I'd say so." The word "fate" gave her pause.

"'Tis a pity to have a man walk out. My father walked out on my mother. That's why I vowed never to marry."

"Oh, Bridget, even after what I've gone through, I do believe there's someone out there for everyone."

"Maybe if one had centuries to look." Bridget reached up and handed her another tumbler.

"Centuries," Faith repeated, thinking about her strange journey through time. Was it fated?

"You know, Doctor Forrester would do well to leave that little Miss LaDue alone. He needs someone like his late wife, someone with intelligence, a sense of humor, someone loving and caring of his child." She paused, turning to Faith. She met her gaze and her face glowed. Her grin was almost a laugh. "Now that I think of it, he could do well to marry someone like you."

The tumbler shattered on the parquet floor before Faith realized she had dropped it. Shards of broken crystal littered the area at her feet.

"I'm sorry," Faith said, trembling. "I just can't believe what you just said."

Bridget stooped down to inspect the damage. "I only say what I think is true. Ever since I met you, I thought, 'Well, there's a girl for the lonely good doctor'."

"This is preposterous."

"I don't think so. Doctor Forrester finds you mysterious and interesting. It's only a matter of time." Bridget winked.

"Bridget, have you been sneaking brandy again?"

"Only a nip here and there. Not enough to affect my mind." She rose. "I'll go fetch a dustpan and remove the mess."

"And please remove the silly ideas."

Later in the afternoon, before dinner, Faith sat on a wrought–iron bench in the garden. Flipping through an issue of the *Saturday Evening Post*, she drew a breath of the sweet scent of azaleas, cherry blossoms, and rhododendrons. Sunlight filtered through the trees while a comforting breeze caressed her face and hands. Though she was attired in her new black uniform, she removed the coordinating gloves. Willing to abide by society's standards in public, what she did in her private moments was her own business. She just wished she could remove the ground–sweeping linen dress with its high starched collar altogether. The color absorbed the heat and the long sleeves and design prevented air from circulating. It was no wonder women carried vials of smelling salts.

Andrew was lounging on a blanket spread on the lawn waging war with his tin soldiers. Faith was determined, that for at least ten minutes, she'd have some peace and quiet before he made demands. She looked down at the magazine spread on her lap trying to learn more about life in 1906 and trying to block out thoughts of the earthquake. There was really nothing more for her to do but to wait.

"Miss Donahue, is the sky falling yet?" Doctor Forrester asked, startling her from her thoughts.

Looking up to meet his dark gaze and snicker puckering his lips, she arched her brows in irritation. "May I help you, sir?"

"I was just wondering if we were all safe from catastrophe today. It's such a glorious afternoon, I thought, perhaps, I was missing something."

She slammed the magazine closed on her lap and drew a deep breath for restraint.

"I've been trying really hard to take my mind off the inevitable and here you are making me think about it."

"I think it's rather interesting how you've drilled my staff and prepared my home. Not a glass or plate is to be found in a cupboard or cabinet. Not one breakable object is to be found on a shelf or wall. I've been told of the packed crates." He stood before her, stroking his chin with his hand. "The pantry is stocked with dry goods and jugs filled with water. Are my windows to be nailed shut, too, or, perhaps, we'll just bolt the shutters?"

She smiled sweetly just to irk him. "One can never be too prepared."

"For an earthquake and fire that you've dreamed up in your pretty little head?" He cocked his head and chuckled, though his laugh was more scornful than humorous.

"For an event that is to take place in the early hours of tomorrow morning. This is merely the calm before the storm," she warned in a deadpan serious tone, her gaze boring into him.

"You really believe it, don't you?" He was staring.

"I know it."

"I hope you're not frightening my son with details of this?" he asked.

She pointed to Andrew, intense at play. "Does he look frightened? There's no need in scaring a child."

"At least we agree on something. Miss Donahue, I wish you to, rather I order you, to refrain from panicking my household staff. My home is being turned into a fort. Tomorrow, I want my belongings returned to their rightful places. I want apologies from you, and…I want your resignation. I will not have my home held hostage by your pandemonium." His lip curled back as he said the words.

She stood to meet him, face-to-face. "Doctor, what will you say or do if my predictions are true? If I have, indeed, saved you and your home from harm, where would I stand? If I'm right, will I be guaranteed a full-time position as governess?"

"It will not happen." He stood firm, like a solid oak.

"It will happen. What will you say? What will you do?"

His face turned crimson, his eyes heated to black. "I have the mind to make you leave now!"

    "Sir?" she asked, unwavering.

    "I am looking forward to tomorrow!"

    He abruptly turned and stalked toward the house.

    Faith sighed. Tomorrow.

CHAPTER 7

THE TORMENT OF AWAITING IMPENDING disaster was almost too much to bear. Faith sat in her bed, fully dressed, hugging her knees to her chest. The seconds ticked into minutes as she stared at her bedside clock.

After a hearty, yet unusually quiet, dinner with Bridget, she retreated up to her room. She needed rest knowing that the coming hours would require all her strength and a clear head.

This wasn't her first experience with earthquakes, she kept reminding herself. Tremors were a common occurrence, something one expected, when living on fault lines in San Francisco. A few broken dishes, an occasional traffic jam, the safety drills in her classroom, the momentary panic were a way of life.

Soothsayers had been warning about the "big one" for years, always citing the 1906 earthquake as an example. Faith always felt that the odds were in her favor that she'd never experience the "big one" in her lifetime. Never in her wildest nightmares did she ever imagine that she would go back in time to experience the original "big one." Even now she kept hoping that she would awaken from this warped nightmare.

Many a night she would lie in bed praying to return. Try as she might to squeeze her eyes shut and chant like Dorothy in the *Wizard of Oz* that "there's no place like home" with hopes of returning to 2006, nothing happened. Whatever weird force propelled her back in time to 1906 seemed intent on keeping her there.

All she could do was brace herself for the inevitable. She quivered with the knowledge that this home would be safe while others would tumble like building blocks and others burn to the ground. Some people would die, others suffer permanent injury, and there was nothing she could do. She knew that she couldn't change history without changing the future. If every resident were warned and heeded her advice, the outcome of the quake and fire would impact future generations, good and bad. She could only sit back helplessly and allow history to happen.

The house was eerily quiet, as if her foreboding had affected everyone. Bridget had been unusually quiet and fidgety between swigs of brandy. Doctor Forrester ignored her completely, busying himself with visiting homebound patients. He even insisted on tucking Andrew in bed.

This evening, the doctor had a dinner engagement with Miss LaDue and box tickets to the Grand Opera House. He was anxious to hear Enrico Caruso open the opera season with the Metropolitan Grand Opera Company. Faith wished that she could have been in Miss LaDue's place to hear history's greatest tenor. The performance would have taken her mind off the impending sense of doom for a few hours. She was certain she would have appreciated Caruso's talent more than the ditsy Miss LaDue.

Once again, thoughts of Brad entered her mind. He and his blonde were probably thrilled to have her out of their lives. Having her out of the way would mean no dueling lawyers, court dates, and alimony.

She had been so upset when he asked for a divorce that she thought her life was over. The reality was that her marriage was over, not her life. In retrospect, her marriage had been over long ago but she had been too blind to notice. Affairs didn't just happen. Handsome, fast–living, smooth–talking attorneys like Brad were never content with one of anything. She knew that he was as devious outside the courtroom as he was within and that he used people his entire life to get what he wanted. Didn't he, after all, use her? After marrying him she had put her life on hold for him. She had been so caught up in the elite lifestyle that she helped to create that she paid little attention to the personal side of their relationship. Brad had never been affectionate, a once–a–day kiss and sex when he was in the mood, holding hands just to show off in front of friends. They led such separate lives for so long that she ignored the writing on the wall. Their life together had been nothing but a public façade.

Without the mementos to jog her memory, the familiar furniture and people, there were no reminders of the life they shared. Being in this strange, new world was like starting over. The weird thing, she realized, was that she hadn't missed Brad. She had been too busy finding herself.

Yawning, she laid back in her narrow bed, on top of the coverlet, her head on a goose–down pillow. She curled up in a comforting fetal position and fell asleep, a dream swirling in her subconscious.

Amidst the scented wildflowers in a fog–shrouded meadow, a man and a woman danced. He held her gloved hand against his chest while his other hand encircled her waist in an intimate embrace. The man was attired in formal black tail, the woman in a flowing white gown of satin and lace. The yards of fabric rippled in the gentle breeze created by their graceful waltz. They danced to music only privy to their ears. Out of the fog stepped a child. Upon seeing him, the couple stopped dancing and turned their heads to face him.

Faith awakened with a startled gasp. The woman's face was her own, the man Doctor Ian Forrester, the child Andrew. She shook her head wondering if it had any significance and figured it didn't make sense. Why was the doctor dancing with her instead of Miss LaDue? He loved Miss LaDue and despised her. She drew a deep breath to cleanse her mind.

The clock chimed. She cast a glance at its face: 4:15 a.m. and trembled, feeling cold and clammy. In one hour the earthquake would shake and forever change the city.

After seeing Andrew's innocent face in the dream, she decided to check on him and sit at his bedside to comfort him when he awakened during the earthquake. A child should not be alone during such a traumatic event and she felt obligated to assure his safety.

She lit the candle in her brass candlestick, entered the hall, and descended the back stairs to the second floor. On tiptoes, as to not disturb the household, she glided down the hall to his room. She gingerly opened his bedroom door and stepped inside. With a flicker of candlelight she surveyed his bed.

"Andrew?" She gasped at the sight of his neatly made, unrumpled bed. There was no sign of the child.

With her heart thumping, she raced from his room and out into the hall. She almost crashed into Bridget in her panic. The maid was staggering down the hall.

"Faith Donahue, you put a fright into me," Bridget scolded, slurring her words.

"Where's Andrew?" Faith asked, breathless.

"Now, now, don't you be worrying. Doctor Forrester's taking care of him."

The scent of brandy was strong. Bridget had been hitting the bottle, rather, emptying it.

"Oh, good, he's in his father's room. He's safe." Faith was relieved.

It was short–lived.

"Oh no, ma'am. Andrew's not home. Neither is the…" she hiccoughed "good doctor."

"What are you saying?" she asked, grabbing Bridget's shoulders with clawed fingers and shaking her.

"Doctor Forrester took Andrew to Miss LaDue's home tonight."

"Why?"

"He feared you would harm his son with all your earthquake talk."

"It isn't talk!" She released her grip on Bridget. She should have known that he'd think her unstable enough to cause harm.

She also knew that she would be getting the last laugh if they survived this. "Where's Andrew?"

"Nob Hill."

"Nob Hill, let me think." Faith closed her eyes for a second, trying to remember local history. Okay, Nob Hill survived the earthquake unscathed only to be dynamited later to stop the raging fire. Andrew would be safe. Thank God the doctor wasn't betrothed to someone in the South of Market shantytown.

"You're certain Andrew's on Nob Hill?"

"Tucked in bed as surely as he would be at home." Bridget hiccoughed again. "I talked on the telephone to Myrna, the La-Due's housekeeper. She assured me that Andrew and the good doctor are fine."

"Okay, okay. Andrew's safe. The doctor's safe," Faith assured herself.

Bridget may have been tipsy but, at least, she had her faculties. Andrew would be safe but the loss would be hers. Faith wouldn't have him to comfort and cling to when the earth trembled. She would be alone.

She wondered where the doctor would be. Was Constance the virginal ice princess she appeared to be? Or was the doctor keeping her comfortable? Faith wondered why she even cared. What the doctor did was his business. Yet, that strange dream replayed in her mind. Why was he dancing with her?

"I need some fresh air," Faith said. She was shaking and the earth had yet to move.

Casting a glance at Bridget, she realized that the woman wouldn't even feel the earthquake. Bridget was already teetering.

As Faith stepped out on to the front porch, a rush of mild and misty air stroked her face. She drew a deep breath trying to subdue frayed nerves. She leaned against a wooden porch post watching as a rosy dawn broke through the fog that drove in from the Bay. The neighborhood was quiet with the restful calm that always seemed to precede tragedy.

Slowly, the city was awakening from a peaceful slumber. Wood smoke from the morning's first fires curled out of brick chimneys scenting the air with wood perfume. Faith knew that servants were stoking the fires to begin a day that would be far from ordinary.

The first shock came without warning. Except for a slight reverberating roar, the earth began to quietly shift. Beneath the porch, the earth began to undulate from east to west. Faith swayed as if she was on roller skates trying to stay standing. She sunk to the wooden porch floor, hugging the porch post for security as well as for support. A queasy ache, like being on an amusement park ride, rose from her stomach.

"I'm safe," she mumbled aloud. "Pacific Heights is built on bedrock. I'm safe."

The earth began to rumble and vibrate. A sickening sensation of heaving ground appeared as the shock increased in intensity. She watched the surrounding landscape sway. Trees bent like palms in a hurricane. The house rattled on its concrete foundation. She shook, wondering how much of the shaking she felt were nerves and how much was the actual earthquake. When the street lamps dimmed, she knew that the gas lines feeding from the central city had ruptured. The fire wouldn't be far behind. She crouched against the porch rails waiting for the tremors to cease.

After a moment of calm and silence, Faith eased herself up to her feet, using the porch post for support. Her legs were weak, as if made of rubber. Sea legs on dry land. Soon, she heard voices as bewildered neighbors ran out of their homes and into the streets. Stepping off the porch, Faith walked down the stone path to the gatepost.

She watched as husbands and wives, servants, and children meandered in the streets, oblivious to being attired in nightclothes and in various states of undress. For all the trembling, there had been little damage to Sacramento Street. A few fallen bricks, displaced objects, and snapped lamp posts seemed of little concern to residents. Their little corner of the world was safe until time revealed the mass destruction just a few blocks away.

Faith unlatched the gate and gingerly stepped out in to the street, as if expecting it to swallow her up at any moment. She strode down the street to survey damage and to catch a glimpse of the destruction down below.

As the sun finally broke through the mist, many residents gathered to look out over the business district from atop their hill. Excited chatter and laughter stopped as if a plug had been pulled. Faces that had been smiling were slack-jawed. The realizations of the extent of the devastation played out like a Nickelodeon show flickering before them.

Off in the distance, fires raged, engulfing their beloved city in fierce orange flames and thick, acrid smoke. The rays of the rising sun competed with the flames angrily greeting the morning. Sheets of fire burst out from the warehouse district near the waterfront, to the business district, Hayes Valley, and the old mission area. Doomed buildings were silhouetted against hungry flames eager to devour them.

As Faith walked down the hill, refugees were making their way up with only the clothes on their backs and squealing children in tow. The pallor of their faces, the blank, glazed look in their eyes revealed their close escape. Fear permeated the air like a new dense fog settling in.

Faith watched the residents retreat into their fine undamaged homes, their refuge from the tragedy befalling their poorer, less fortunate neighbors. Faith knew that she should be returning to check on Bridget and to secure the doctor's home. Desperate people did desperate things. She remembered reading about looting after the quake. She wondered if the worst was over or if the worst had just begun.

A sense of helplessness and empathy permeated her being. Reading about the earthquake and being forewarned had done little to prepare her for the reality of it. The sounds of crackling timber in the distance, echoing cries of suffering and death, seeing the hollow and blank eyes, the pungent scent of a burning hell penetrating more than her nostrils.

She was about ready to turn around and run toward 92 Sacramento Street when she saw him approaching in the distance. With Andrew perched on his shoulders, the doctor appeared unscathed. Her heart skipped a beat as they drew near. Would Doctor Forrester finally believe her?

When he noticed her, he quickened his pace.

"You knew! You knew about this! You were right!" he yelled in a voice filled with surprise, guilt, and the admission of defeat.

Andrew waved his little hands as if he wanted to fly away and greet her. He was smiling. The innocence of children was to be buffeted from life's tragedies.

"Miss Donahue!" the little boy screamed.

"Andrew! Doctor! You're safe!" she replied, running to greet them. Faith smiled with the knowledge that they all survived. She wondered if securing their safety was the reason for her sudden appearance in their lives. The thought gave her pause.

As they drew near, the doctor's eyes met hers. The intensity of his gaze was riveting, almost hypnotic. She stopped in her tracks.

Doctor Forrester looked at her, wanting to apologize for his being a "doubting Thomas." She was right in predicting the earthquake and fire. She had been concerned enough to secure his home, stockpile provisions, and provide for the safety of his household.

There was something beyond strange and unusual in the woman. She wasn't insane but harbored knowledge beyond the realm of normal human understanding. He had to get to the bottom of her gift for prophecy and her claim to be from some future world. The scientist in him was curious. The man in him was mystified.

She also had a way with children. Andrew whimpered all night, crying out for her even as he slept nestled in his father's arms. A father's love wasn't enough. He had hoped that Miss LaDue would fill the void left by the child's mother. Constance, though, had shown little interest in the boy. He hoped that her attitude would change when they married. If not, he thought how Miss Donahue could help. He had grown up with a governess and had fond memories.

He had held his son all night as he slept knowing that he needed comfort as much as the boy. An unsettling feeling had kept him awake all night checking the clock on the mantel in the LaDue's guestroom.

He wanted to think that Faith's warnings were the nonsensical ravings of a mad woman. As the hours passed, though, he was on edge. At the first rumblings of the quake he cuddled his son to his chest. They rode out the trembling waves, bouncing on the mattress as if on a boat in a storm–tossed sea. He calmed Andrew by comparing the earthquake experience to that of the fun rides at the amusement park. As the paintings, objects d'art, tumbled to the floor and chaos erupted in the LaDue household, he held on to Andrew.

Only when the shaking ceased did he believe they were safe. They emerged from the bedroom into a home of hysterical women. Constance's mother had collapsed on the sofa in one of her "spells." Her husband frantically held smelling salts up to her nose while a servant fanned her. Constance was prone on the fainting couch being attended to by her maid. He imagined the scene being played out in most of the other Nob Hill mansions. As a physician, there was nothing more for him to do than hand hold the matrons.

When he stepped out of the house and observed the chaos erupting in the city below, he knew that his services were needed in a more critical way. People were dying out there. He could hear the shrill cries of pain and suffering, could see the damage and the dancing flames. He had a professional and a human obligation to enter the fray to help in any way possible. As he checked on his motorcar parked in front of the massive stone and stucco mansion, a policeman approached.

"Are things as bad as they appear?" the doctor asked the young policeman who seemed ill prepared for such a cataclysmic event. His eyes burned dark and damp with fear.

"Worse, much worse. The gas lines ruptured feeding a fire that's spread through the business district."

"Surely, the fire department?"

"The main water mains busted, only a trickle in the taps. Chief Sullivan's dead, killed as he slept in the firehouse. The cupola from the California Hotel went right through the roof. There's panic in the streets. So many displaced people, dead, and injured. Looters are beginning to take advantage."

The doctor shook his head.

"We might be needing that motorcar, sir. Words come down to confiscate motorcars and horse teams to aid in rescue efforts. All hell's broken loose and we need all the help we can get."

"I'm a doctor and am prepared to do what I can."

"Then you'll be needing the motorcar."

"My feet can carry me. There are others out there who are not so fortunate. Transportation might make the difference between life and death. Please, take the motorcar."

"Are you certain?"

"Yes, I can walk."

He had the sudden urge to return to his home on Sacramento Street. He had to return there to pick up his doctor's satchel and supplies and decided that it would be the best place for Andrew to be. The boy needed familiar surroundings at a time like this. At the LaDue's he would be ignored and alone. In his home he would have Faith to watch over him.

He suspected that his home and its contents were secure, thanks to Faith. Faith.

He snapped out of his thoughts and watched Faith run toward them, her drab skirt billowing, tendrils escaping from her unkempt pompadour, her graceful arms flailing, her complexion aglow in the morning mist, her eyes like glittering sapphires. He wondered why he hadn't noticed any of this before. He had spent so much time ridiculing her that he never really paid attention to her. He looked at her as if for the very first time.

Without any warning, another tremor, weaker than the first, rocked the earth. After instilling panic to the panic-stricken, it stopped as quickly as it began.

"Faith!" the doctor warned, scrambling to get to her.

She looked up to see a concrete gargoyle sailing through the air, ornamentation displaced from a rooftop. As she turned to get out of harm's way she felt the sharp pain of impact. Darkness swallowed up the pain as she drifted out of consciousness.

CHAPTER 8

FAITH'S HEAD ACHED AS IF it was being squeezed in a vice while being banged on top with a sledgehammer. The pain throbbed with such excruciating agony that she hoped it could be cut out of her skull, anything for relief. As she attempted to raise her head it felt so heavy that even a slight movement made her dizzy.

She tried to open her eyes but they felt as if they were being held down by lead weights. When she tried to speak, her lips were numb. Her entire body was feeble and immobile. The only alert sense was her hearing. She needed to hear familiar sounds for evidence of her being alive and not in some altered state of being. The sounds she heard were mechanical pumps; the swoosh of rushing air, and intermittent electronic beeps. The sounds were unmistakable. She had been in a hospital before.

Her mind was foggy and filled with strange images dancing in her mind. Vignettes of disconnected scenes, like jumbled movie previews, appeared: a red Jaguar sinking, a tall man elegantly attired in formal black, a little boy snapping a slingshot, a teetering Irish maid, the ground rumbling, and trees swaying. The visions were both a comfort and an irritation. She squirmed, the ability to move her limbs offering a sense of relief. She softly moaned.

"Nurse! Nurse!" a familiar woman's voice frantically called.

Faith turned her head toward the sound. Heavy footsteps bounded in, shoes squeaking as they drew near.

"She seems to be snapping out of it," the familiar woman's

voice said in breathless excitement.

"It's hard to say with head injury cases. Each one is unique," the other husky, unfamiliar female voice replied.

"She was moving and making sounds."

"Let's see if she does it again. Why don't you try talking to her?"

"Faith, Faith. This is Clarice. Remember me? We've been so worried about you. We thought we lost you. Come on, honey, say something. Do something. Let me know that you're gonna be okay," she pleaded.

A recollection of she and another woman sipping Chardonnay in a swanky hilltop restaurant entered Faith's mind. The other woman was…

"Clar–ice," Faith formed the words in a strained whisper.

"Yes! Yes!" Clarice squealed.

Faith eased her eyes open until they captured the image of a statuesque African–American woman looking down at her. Clarice's wide, ivory grin lit up her caramel face.

Long wild hair, "Diana Ross hair," as Faith had called it, framed her strong, angular bone structure. Tears streamed from her ebony eyes as they caught Faith's.

"Praise God, you're out of the coma!" Clarice shouted, raising her arms and looking up at the ceiling. "I've been praying for your recovery so often, it's about time God listened."

Faith cracked a smile at the sight of her best friend. She still was hazy and confused.

"What…what happened to me?" Faith asked.

Clarice looked at her. "That's a good question. You're the only one who can provide the answer."

"I have a horrible, pounding headache." The pain continued to grip Faith's skull.

"I'll get the doctor," the nurse, who stood nearby, said.

"The doctor?" Faith asked. "Doctor Forrester?"

The nurse cocked her curly gray head. "There's no one by that name here." After casting a glance at Clarice, she turned and walked out into the hall.

"Doctor Forrester?" Faith repeated. She closed her eyes and for a fleeting moment the towering figure of a darkly handsome yet arrogant man flashed in her mind.

"Mrs. Donahue," a man asked, startling her from her thoughts.

She opened her eyes. The slick black hair and the title "Doctor" stitched his white lab coat was all the men had in common, she decided.

"I'm Doctor Chan," he introduced, squinting his slanted eyes beneath thick eyeglasses. You are one lucky woman." He removed a stethoscope from his lab coat pocket. "Where did you get that nasty gash on your head?"

"The...the earthquake," the words escaping from her lips.

"What earthquake?" he asked.

"The big one."

"No earthquake here, big or small." He chuckled.

Clarice, who had stepped aside to let the doctor check on his patient, shifted on her feet and cleared her throat.

The doctor turned to her. "Probably the head injury."

Clarice nodded.

The doctor turned his attention back to Faith. He set the chestpiece of the stethoscope against her chest, moving it up and down the front of her hospital gown, the earpiece plugged in his ears. As his stubby fingers brushed her, she could remember another's hands. Doctor Forrester's slender fingers were like a gentle caress as he held a chestpiece against her. She tingled and then shivered at the memory.

Doctor Chan removed the stethoscope and shoved it in his lab coat pocket. From another pocket, he withdrew a pen–light.

"How did I come...back?" Faith mumbled.

The doctor arched his brows, forming bushy triangles. "You were comatose for four days."

"How did I come back from...there?" she asked, a vague memory of being in a different place and time, far removed from the modern technology that surrounded her.

The doctor bent over her. With one hand he held open her eyelid, with the other he flashed a beam of light. He repeated the process in the other eye. Content with his inspection, he turned out the light and stuck it in his pocket.

"How did I come back?" she asked again.

Doctor Chan cast a glance at Clarice and winked.

"Head injuries will cause strange thoughts and actions. She'll be fine in a week or two. As the brain contusions shrink and disappear, she'll be back to normal."

"Faith's never been normal." Clarice smiled.

"None of us are," the doctor answered with a smirk. "I'll check on the patient again tomorrow morning. In the meantime, I'll have the nurse give her some Demerol."

Faith watched the doctor shuffle out of the room.

Clarice stepped toward Faith's bedside, pulling up a nearby chair. She slunk her big–boned frame in it and sat facing Faith.

"You're gonna be just fine. You gave us quite a scare."

"I did?"

"You did. Jeez, at first I thought you up and killed yourself. When I saw your car being pulled out of the Bay on the ten o'clock news, I almost died myself. My Reggie said that I almost turned white. Anyway, some restaurant employee said he saw your car roll off the cliff side parking lot. Police called in divers but there was no…no body," Clarice explained.

"It…it's coming back to me, slowly, but it's coming back. I do remember crashing into the water. I've never been so afraid in my life. Just thinking about it is giving me chills. I…I waited for the car to sink, for the interior to pressurize so I could open the door. I escaped. I swam up to the surface and…and…"

"Yes, yes?" Clarice asked, leaning forward.

"I remember awakening in my bedroom but it wasn't my bedroom. That's when it happened," Faith said, memories of a warped past she couldn't quite comprehend permeating her mind. As the strange thoughts appeared, her headache seemed to peel away at each layer of returning recollection.

"What happened?"

"When I realized that I had gone back in time. That's it! I went back in time! Somehow, I've come back!" She even startled herself at the revelation. Her heart rate increased and she began to hyperventilate.

"Shh…now stay calm." Clarice grabbed Faith's trembling hand.

Faith looked down at the IV plug, the tubing leading from the top of her hand to a plastic bag on a metal stand. Clear nourishment flowed down inside the tube in steady droplets. She stared at them as if they were alien objects and her eyes opened wide.

"Oh, God! I've come back!" she gasped, shutting her eyes.

"You'd better rest now, honey. I'm just glad you're doing better. I've been worried sick." Clarice patted Faith's hand and set it down at her side.

"Clarice?" Faith opened her eyes. "Where was I found?"

"On Sacramento Street, down a ways from your house. You were found lying in the middle of the road covered in blood from a head wound, with no ID. Do you know that your picture was flashed on the news in an appeal to identify you? Here, I thought you drowned in the bay and a few days later I see you on TV. I called in. I'm beginning to think I should just skip watching the news." Clarice stood, smoothing her tailored fuchsia suit.

"Thank you."

"For what, honey?"

"For being here."

"That's what friends are for. Now, you rest."

"I'm so confused." Faith sighed.

Faith was riding on a roller coaster of emotion and confusion. As she lay in her hospital bed, awaiting recovery from the mysterious head injury, she had a hard time separating reality from fantasy. She assured herself that the time travel episodes were fantasy. Clarice explained that people who suffer traumatic injuries often create a world in which to escape the pain and recover.

She just couldn't understand how the world revolving around

Doctor Forrester, Andrew, and Bridget could seem so real. Their faces were so vivid, their voices so distinct in her mind. She could even smell the doctor's spicy scent and the brandy on Bridget's breath. Her imagination had never been so real.

Recalling events, imaginary or real, she wove them into the facts explained by Clarice. Five days had lapsed from the time her car sank in the bay to the morning she was discovered unconscious on Sacramento Street. No one had an explanation as to where she was during that time span. Though she had suffered a deep gash and head injury, there was no weapon or object where she lay. Other facts struck her as more than coincidental when Clarice revealed them.

"You really don't remember much do you?" Clarice asked during a later visit.

"So much is vague and some of it is downright weird."

"Weird? Like the clothes you were wearing when you were found." Clarice frowned, scrunching up her face.

"What was I wearing?"

"Honey, something you wouldn't be caught dead in. Some dowdy long black skirt with a matching shirt–like blouse, orthopedic shoes, and some pouffed chignon hairstyle topped with a frumpy little black frilled hat."

"Oh, no." Faith gasped. It was the ugly black uniform Constance LaDue had chosen for her. "What…what was the date?"

"April 18. Why?" Clarice shrugged her broad shoulders, not understanding the significance.

"The date of the great 1906 earthquake." Faith grew suddenly hot and nauseous. This couldn't be happening. This wasn't possible.

"Yeah, I guess it was."

"I…I was dressed like a governess in 1906 and was found on Sacramento Street on April 18," she said out loud, as much for herself to hear as for Clarice. "It isn't some injury–induced dream, after all. I'm not going crazy. It happened. It really happened."

"What?"

"I went back in time a hundred years and, somehow, I came back."

"I wouldn't be saying that too loud around here," Clarice surveyed the room and the empty hall.

"I'm telling the truth." Faith reached up and grabbed Clarice's arm. "You're my best friend. You have to believe me."

Clarice stared at her. "I want to believe you. I really do. It just doesn't make sense. Then again, none of this makes sense. Ever since Bradley walked out on you, nothing has made sense." She shook her head and stepped back, confused.

"You'll help me?" Faith pleaded.

"With what?"

"With finding out the truth, of proving that I traveled back in time."

"If you believe it, why do you need proof?"

"I have to prove it to myself and have to know why. I need to know where my destiny is."

CHAPTER 9

FAITH HAD SOME UNEXPECTED VISITORS. Detectives from the homicide unit of the San Francisco Police Department had shown unusual interest in the progress of her recovery.

She learned that, to her surprise, they had posted a uniformed patrolman to stand like a sentinel outside the door to her room.

When the lead detective swaggered into her private room, she was startled but not shocked. Clarice warned her about the department's interest in her case.

"Now that you're feeling better, Mrs. Donahue, I thought it's time we had a chat," the plainclothes detective said as he approached her bedside. He had a short Jack Webb–style haircut and even flashed his badge with the same amount of authority and flair.

"Joe Friday, I presume?" Faith asked, not being able to help herself. She forced a smile as she scooted up in her bed.

"Sergeant Schmidt, homicide," he introduced, tucking the badge within his inside suit pocket.

"Whom did I kill?" she asked in a light tone, feeling queasy.

"You didn't kill anyone."

"That's good news." She met his intense steely gray gaze.

"You're the one I thought had died."

"Oh?" She had this sinking feeling in the pit of her stomach that gravitated to her face.

"Your husband's sitting in jail under suspicion of murder, your murder," he said in a no–nonsense tone that matched his facial expression, or lack of it.

"Brad?" She gasped.

"Bradley Clark Donahue III."

She shook her head, a shiver crawling up her spine. "I don't understand."

"I think you know a lot more than you're saying. You don't have to be afraid of him. He's under lock and key. There's enough evidence to keep him there. You're even guarded."

"I know."

"What happened the day and evening when your car ended up in San Francisco Bay?"

"I don't remember much."

"Try. What did you and Bradley discuss? Was he angry?"

She hesitated. "He told me that he didn't love me any more and that he wanted a divorce." The words made her more angry than sad and she looked down at her hands. The wedding ring wasn't on her finger. Just as well, she didn't need a reminder of Bradley and their sham of a marriage.

"Was he violent? Did he threaten you?"

"Brad never used physical violence. He's more a man of words."

"Did he know your destination the night you met Clarice at the restaurant, the night your car rolled off the cliff?"

"I don't think so." She looked up at him. "Why?"

"Murder. Now, attempted murder," Detective Schmidt said, enunciating the words with seething under his breath.

"What makes you think Bradley was trying to kill me?" She knew that Bradley was capable of many things, but murder?

"For one thing, a mysterious clutch problem with your car." He raised a bushy eyebrow, checking her reaction.

She swallowed hard. "My car?"

"When we pulled it out of the bay, we had the car thoroughly inspected. It was discovered that your clutch had been tampered with."

"Oh no!" She drew her hands up to her ashen face. "Bradley. He had the car serviced the day before the...mishap."

The detective nodded with a glimmer in his eyes. "Did you know about the life insurance policy?"

"The what?" she asked, fearing what revelation the detective might uncover next.

"Seems that Bradley took out a million–dollar life insurance policy on you a few months ago, with a double indemnity clause. You know, in case of accidental death."

This was beginning to sound like a classic Alfred Hitchcock movie. She was cold, clammy, and faint. If the heart monitor hadn't been disconnected, she was certain it would have gone off.

"I…I—"

"There's more." He smirked.

"More?"

"What do you know about Mr. Donahue's business practices? About his clients?"

"I…I really don't know much. He's a partner in a big litigation firm handling injury claims, personal lawsuits, some defense, and some corporate stuff. His job was basically his business and he rarely discussed it with me…always said he had enough of it at the office and wanted it left there." Just as he had left his paramour there, she realized. Two separate lives.

"I just wish wives would take a more active role in their husband's affairs. There would be less work for the detective bureau and the courts." He shrugged his shoulders, and continued, "Mr. Donahue has been under investigation for his involvement with the mob."

"The mob?"

"Been doing a little consulting for them. The way I figure it, he had one of their goons try to do you in."

"You're kidding?"

"No ma'am."

"I…I thought it was a freak accident."

"Nothing in this world is ever accidental. Mind if I take a seat?"

"Help yourself." She pointed to a white resin chair.

Detective Schmidt eased himself into the chair with a sigh. His burly form just fit. He sat for a moment analyzing her.

"One mystery remains. What happened to you after your car ended up in the bay?" he asked.

"After?"

"You see, witnesses at the restaurant said they saw a woman behind the wheel of the car as it plunged over the cliff. Was that woman really you?"

"Yes," she answered without hesitation. She proceeded to explain her escape from the sinking car. "The last thing I remember is thinking how peaceful the night was when I surfaced."

"Remember anything else?" His eyes bore into her.

She hesitated, wondering whether she should mention the unusual experience of going back in time to 1906. After all, it was her only explanation for the time lapse. One look at Detective Schmidt's stoic face made her realize how absurd it would sound. She wasn't even sure if she believed it herself.

"No," she replied, staring into his eyes, wanting him to believe her. "I just remember waking up in this hospital room after some sort of head injury."

CHAPTER 10

THE PHRASE, "GOING HOME" SEEMED silly. In a way Faith felt she had been home all along, just 100 years earlier. The short ride from Presbyterian Medical Center to 92 Sacramento Street was a time of reflection. The contrast of grand old Victorian homes set against the city's backdrop of skyscrapers was much like the way she felt. A hundred years earlier, no one would have imagined the towering Transamerica pyramid just as she would not have envisioned going back in time. She sighed, if she had gone back in time.

Clarice navigated the Camry into a tight space in front of the house. Faith rolled down the window and gazed out at the Queen Anne Victorian with its loft gables, conical roof tower, ornamentation, and expansive front porch. Goosebumps traveled up her arms as she looked in admiration at the grand old lady. The house was as pristine as in her prime. The gray and mauve color scheme she had selected a few years earlier, she realized, was original to the home.

The one thing that was not original was the police car parked in front, assigned to protect her while the investigation into her accident was resolved.

"Well, ready to go in?" Clarice asked, a pensive smile on her face.

"Sure," Faith replied, taking a deep breath for confidence. Thoughts of Brad and the mob made her hesitate.

Clarice reached over and patted Faith's trembling hand. They had been friends a long time, through both good times and bad. This time seemed like a mixture of both.

"Like they say, 'there's no place like home'." Clarice opened her door and slid out of her seat.

Slamming her door shut, she moved around to Faith's side and opened the passenger side door. She leaned over and offered her hand.

"I'm not an invalid, you know." Faith met her concerned narrow gaze.

"I just want to help."

Trying to ease herself out of the passenger seat, Faith realized how weak she really was. Her legs were heavy as if weighted down with concrete, her head was light and dizzy. She reached up to grasp Clarice's hand and let her help pull her up and out of the automobile. She clung as Clarice closed the car door and led her to toward the front gate. Unlatching the picket gate, they ambled, arm–in–arm up the front brick walk.

Faith glanced at the yard. The garden she had tended sprouted multicolored azaleas, bougainvillea, and crisp daffodils. Cherry trees stood in fragrant bloom. She shook her bandaged head, hidden beneath a floppy cloth hat. Even the scent was eerily familiar of another springtime either real or imagined.

As they stepped up on the front porch, Faith surveyed the antique white wicker furniture and hanging swing, the puffy floral cushions, the hanging baskets of ferns, and pots of scarlet geraniums.

"Doctor Forrester didn't have any furniture on the porch. It looks so much nicer with than without," Faith whispered.

"Who? What?" Clarice asked.

"Brad hated this porch," Faith mumbled.

"He liked all that funky contemporary stuff."

"Yeah, and I always liked antiques."

"Opposites always seem to attract."

"With disastrous results," Faith said, thinking about Brad and what the detective had implied. "The key's under the mat."

"The what?" Their eyes met.

"The key. I always keep an extra under the front doormat." Faith pointed to the glossy wooden floor.

"Under the mat? That isn't safe."

Faith shrugged her shoulders. "I figure, because it's such an obvious place, a thief would overlook it."

She stooped down, turned up the doormat, and removed the brass key. She stood, smoothing her linen slacks.

"See, I haven't forgotten everything." Faith winked.

Clarice jiggled the key in the heavy brass lock, pushed, pulled, and opened the heavy oak door rattling its leaded glass insert.

As she stepped into the foyer, Faith felt as if she had stepped into a stranger's home. The uncluttered contemporary design and sparse furnishings seemed as though they belonged to someone else. She closed her eyes, remembering how the house should have been.

"Oh, Bridget," she murmured.

Clarice helped her upstairs to her bedroom, another alien environment filled with cold chrome, brass, and glass. After tucking Faith in the squishy waterbed, Clarice placed a steaming cup of tea on the glass and brass nightstand, and deposited a book on her bed. Somehow *Midnight in the Garden of Good and Evil* didn't seem appropriate. Clarice sighed. Maybe it was too appropriate under the circumstances. Faith looked up at her like a sick child needing reassurance and Clarice smiled.

"Now, you rest. Remember if you need anything, give me a call," Clarice said, pointing to the phone on the nightstand. "I'll come back tomorrow morning with some groceries."

"Yes, ma'am," Faith saluted. "Go home to your family. I'm sure Reggie and the kids need you more than I do. You've done enough for me already."

"I'm just being a friend, that's all. Now, you just behave yourself and stay put."

"Don't worry. I do intend to stay in this century, for now." She winked.

Faith watched Clarice sashay out of the room. She listened as her footsteps faded down the hall, the front staircase, and foyer. She heard the door close and the lock click.

Clarice was the closest she had to family. Thoughts of how Brad made her move to California, away from her parents, made her bitter. Syracuse was far from San Francisco and their visits had been few and far between. She was alone then. Now that they were gone, she was more alone than ever.

She closed her eyes. She didn't know when she drifted off to sleep. Images whirled through her mind like an ever-changing kaleidoscope.

The earth trembled beneath her feet, causing her to dance against her will. Hungry cracks opened in the street anxious to gobble up everything in its wake. She shrieked in blood-curdling terror as the earth heaved and buildings toppled over like children's building blocks. Other screams pierced the angry dawn. Mutterings of disbelief followed and than, silence. Tears streamed down faces of young and old, rich and poor as they watched orange flames engulfing the rubble and turning it into a fiery hell. The ocean's breeze billowed the smoke, causing the flames to leap and dance from building to building.

She looked up and saw them.

Their faces were as vivid as a Technicolor movie.

Black curls framed an innocent cherub face, a pudgy finger stuck in a rosebud mouth, twinkling dark eyes focused on her. Nestled in his father's arms, Andrew reached out to her.

"Miss Donahue!" the child cried.

Doctor Forrester held on tight to the boy. Eyes that were glazed over in fear and disbelief gazed at her, questioning, wondering.

"You knew! You knew! You were right!" he screamed.

As he moved toward her, he called out, "Faith! Faith!"

Suddenly, he froze in his tracks. His mouth gaped open, his eyes wide as if he had seen something unfathomable.

"Faith! Faith, come back!" His voice was a muffled cry that grew louder and clearer. "Faith, come back!"

She awakened shivering in a cold sweat, his dusky voice resonating in her mind. Reaching up to swipe beads of perspiration from her forehead, she whispered, "Doctor Forrester. Dearest Andrew."

The two figures seemed too real to be a figment of her imagination. She tried to rethink the scene that had just flashed in her mind. What did the doctor witness? Had she, indeed, traveled back in time, she would have returned after having been struck in the head during the tremor. He would have seen her vanish right before his eyes. Not only had she told him about her coming from the future, warned him about the earthquake and fire, but disappeared in an instant. She reasoned that it had to have been a frightening scene. People just don't disappear like characters in *Star Trek* being "beamed up." Even though he was a scientific man, she knew he wouldn't have an explanation. She just left without a trace.

She drew a deep breath to calm her frazzled nerves and slowly exhaled. Was her brain still playing tricks on her or did this Doctor Forrester really exist? The sooner she uncovered the truth, the better.

CHAPTER 11

BEING HOME REQUIRED MORE OF an adjustment than Faith anticipated. As she regained her strength, she explored the house from cellar to attic. She paced each room, her mood melancholy and ill at ease. Everything was wrong. The furnishings were inappropriate, stark, and uninviting. The home's true character lay hidden beneath layers of wallpaper, wall–to–wall carpeting, and shiny chrome fixtures. Rich architectural detail and moldings were disguised or painted over. The home reminded her of a center for contemporary art; a museum of Dakota furniture, Dali prints, freeform sculpture, and neutral hues.

The house was like Brad: cold. She hugged herself to warm the shiver that tingled down her spine.

Her mind held a snapshot of how each room was supposed to look. She envisioned the home's interior restored to its original cluttered Victorian splendor. As she stood in the front parlor, she noted the carved mantel. Thoughts of warm wood and jewel tones, thick fabric, plush rugs, scattered pillows, and lacy plants filled her mind. She could picture a lived–in house where a little boy could scamper and where his father could read sunken in a worn leather chair. She wanted the home to exude a comfort she once knew. She sought her own place to call home.

Floor–by–floor and piece–by–piece, she shoved the modern furniture out into the halls. Beginning in her bedroom, she crawled on the floor on her hands and knees. At the perimeter of the room, she pried up the carpeting from the tacking strips. Each yank revealed the polished wooden floor hidden underneath. She rolled up the carpet and pushed it in the center of the room. After, she peeled the neutral wallpaper from the walls. She clawed at it, getting personal satisfaction from each rip and shred. When the paper was removed, she collapsed on the wooden floor finding strange comfort in the wood and the bare walls.

When Clarice stopped by, her eyes bulged at the sight of Faith's home. Each room was in total disarray. Carpeting was rolled up, wallpaper peeled off, furniture piled up like discarded refuse. Amidst all of the chaotic mess, Faith sat smiling with contentment. She was proud of her handiwork and wore it like a badge of valor.

"What the hell…" Clarice began, stepping over materials in the parlor.

"Isn't it exciting?" Faith was beaming and giggling like a schoolgirl.

"It's a mess. Your house used to look like a feature in *Metropolitan Home*. Now, look at it."

"This is just the beginning," Faith said, standing. She brushed paper shreds off her tattered jeans and faded sweatshirt.

"Of what?"

She met Clarice's stunned gaze. "Of what this home was meant to be. I'm going to return it to what it once was. In 1906 it was splendorous. None of this contemporary trash."

"Trash? Honey, this stuff is expensive." Clarice surveyed the furniture chosen by one of the city's finest interior designers. Brad had spared no expense on the house.

"I'm selling this furniture and all the accessories. The sooner it's out of here, the better."

Clarice placed her hands on her hips and looked at Faith. "I see. You want Bradley's influence out of your life."

"I just want my life."

"By the way, there's a part of your old life you forgot about. Remember, I was supposed to be driving you to the Civic Center to see Bradley. You know, the preliminary hearing?"

"Oh, do I have to?" Faith let out an audible sigh, though she hadn't forgotten.

"Yes or else you might not end up with enough money to complete your rehab project."

"I'm such a mess. I'll have to get dressed." She rushed out in the foyer to the stairs.

"Hurry. And Faith…" Clarice began.

Faith turned to face her, one hand on the newel post.

"Next time you need help, my Reggie is pretty handy."

Faith knew that confronting Bradley would be one of the toughest challenges she'd have to meet. The last time she saw him was at breakfast on that ill-fated day.

"I don't love you any more. I want a divorce." The words came back, repeating themselves over and over in her head.

At that time, she was facing an imminent divorce. Little did she realize that Brad would be facing attempted murder charges as well, her attempted murder. She could see

Brad's divorcing her, but murdering her? She didn't think he was capable of murder. Adultery? Yes.

The prosecutors and defense reluctantly agreed with the judge to allow Faith to meet with Bradley alone. Faith's lawyer, Clarice's brother, smirked when she made her request. He commented that her appearance was like Lazarus rising from the dead.

When she hesitated in the doorway before entering the paneled office, Brad's eyes bulged as if she had been resurrected. As she entered the room, she met his intense gaze. To think that those dark eyes used to make her heart flutter. Now, they just left her frozen. Deep crow's feet lined the corners, frown lines imbedded in his forehead and chin as if chiseled in. His auburn hair shone with specks of gray. Stress aged the man. Instead of being shocked, she was pleased.

She pulled out a wooden chair across from him at the small

round conference table and sat facing him. She sat erect, tall, and firm, facing him as if he were an opponent in a chess tournament.

"Thank God, you're alive," Brad said and sighed. "They thought I killed you."

She maintained a steady gaze, looking right at him. "You did kill me."

"What are you saying?" he asked, leaning into the table.

"That morning, when you said you didn't love me and wanted a divorce. You stabbed me in the heart with your words. You killed my youth, my career dreams, my hope for a family, my dedication as a wife and a partner. You killed me, Brad."

"Oh, come on," he scoffed, raking his hands through his wavy hair.

"You killed me," she repeated, her gaze unwavering and voice firm.

"Come on, Faith, Just tell the police the truth. I never laid a hand on you. You know I didn't." His voice was getting high pitched as it did when he was annoyed.

"Maybe you just hired someone else to do your dirty work, as usual."

He stared at her in silence, his eyes growing darker.

She looked at him as if she were seeing him for the first time. What she had seen as ambition was really greed in disguise. What she had seen as pride had been selfishness. He didn't inquire as to her welfare or her whereabouts. He didn't ask why she was wearing a hat when she had never worn hats. He was only concerned about saving himself. One would display more concern for a pet than he displayed toward her. After all those years of marriage

"Come off it, Faith. What have you been doing, reading detective novels? Why would I want you dead?" He rested his elbows on the table.

"A new wifey, for starters and how about the insurance money?" She was stone-faced.

"Oh, that. If you look into it, I also purchased a policy for myself at the same time." He snickered.

"With a double indemnity clause?"

"Both policies are the same. I swear it."

"What hood did you hire to sabotage my car?"

He made a fist and banged it on the table. "You want the truth, I'll give you the truth. I didn't hire anyone. Dammit, it was meant for me."

"What are you saying?"

His face went scarlet. "They thought it was my car."

The revelation made her feel a bit better, if he was telling the truth. The truth and Brad were an oxymoron. Maybe his mobster clients had a bone to pick with him and decided to take matters in their own hands. Both she and Brad drove identical cars. Mistakes could happen. If that were the case, she surmised that he was probably better off in jail. If he were released it would be open season again. She knew that Brad had more to worry about than a divorce and an attempted murder rap. Not only was his comfy existence at stake but his life as well.

"Faith, tell them the truth and I'll be free."

"Free, huh?" She shook her head.

"I need to get out of here," he said, lowering his voice.

"What about me, Brad?"

"The divorce settlement will take care of you."

"Is that what you think?"

"Faith, stop this nonsense. You know I never wanted to see you dead."

"Do I?" She stood, her gaze focused on him.

Brad jumped out of his chair so fast it fell back to the floor with a thud.

"Come on, Faith!" he pleaded.

As she turned her back to walk away, the door to the office opened. An armed bailiff entered in time to see Brad's lunging hands poised at the back of Faith's neck.

CHAPTER 12

"I'VE NEVER BEEN SO CONFUSED in my entire life," Faith lamented over a cup of cappuccino. She glanced across at Clarice who sat sipping mineral water as the conversations buzzed around them in the cramped coffee shop.

"Honey, we go back quite a ways. You've been confused a lot."

"I know." Faith cracked a smile. "You were my first friend when I arrived in San Francisco."

"You needed a friend. No one in their right mind would have chosen to teach in the Tenderloin." Clarice arched her thin brows.

"The pay was good."

"You were young, white, and all wrong."

"I thought I was right."

"It turned out that way. I couldn't believe your determination and the way you stood up to those hoodlums and gained their respect. I thought, surely, you'd be beaten to a pulp or worse. I wasn't gonna see it happen."

"It didn't. Thanks for being the first staff member and black person to stand up for me. Here you are, standing up for me again."

"Because I know you'd do the same for me. You did help me. Remember how you talked me out of that abusive relationship? Without you I never would've met Reggie."

"He's a good guy, solid like an oak." Faith grinned. Reggie was built like a tree, too. Pumping iron was part of a fireman's routine and he was one of San

Francisco's finest. While speaking to her class on fire safety, Faith introduced him to Clarice. The sparks ignited and after five years and two kids, they were still a loving pair. Faith sighed. If only she was so lucky.

"You know, one day you're gonna meet Mr. Right. Maybe you already have and don't know it." Clarice cupped her hands around her glass.

Faith laughed. She hadn't laughed in a long time and it felt good.

"One thing's for certain, I met Mr. Wrong," Faith said, her smile fading into scorn.

"I still can't believe Brad would want you dead."

"Brad denies it. Claims he was the intended victim. With some of the low lives he deals with I can almost believe it."

"With Brad, anything's possible."

"Brad wouldn't kill me?" Faith looked into Clarice's eyes seeking some assurance.

"He would divorce you." Clarice's gaze was a steadfast as her manner. "You know, silly as it seems, isn't it rather just revenge having him sit in jail after all the hell he's put you through?"

"I'm not a vengeful person." Faith folded her arms on the table in front of her. "Clarice, what are you driving at?"

"If he was my man, I'd keep him in jail for a while. He's an attorney, after all, let him change places with his clients. Make him sweat."

"Unless I step in and prove otherwise, they're holding him as a suspect in my attempted murder."

"And wouldn't you be afraid having him out and about? If he did mess with your car, what could he do next?"

"Clarice, you are so bad, you're good."

Clarice laughed, tossing her fluffy hair over her shoulder. "Been there, done that."

"I do need some time, time to research this belief that I've been back in time." "You really do believe it, don't you?"

"What did you think?"

"That it was the head injury, but now that you're back to normal—"

"Don't say it. I need to research this stuff."

"And if you're wrong?"

"What if I'm right?"

Faith gathered a spiral notebook, pencils and pens in her leather attaché and made a visit to the Main Public Library. She hoped that amongst the heaving shelves of musty old books, yards of microfilm, and yellowed archival photographs she would find the answers to the questions that nagged at her mind.

A craggy librarian, who looked old enough to have experienced the great earthquake firsthand, was eager to offer assistance. Harry considered himself an expert on "the big one" and "the great fire" and was more than willing to share his knowledge and research. He and Faith hunched over stacks of books, poring over dusty pages, seeking information. Book after book on early San Francisco, books that had survived the catastrophe, some with leather binding that had been singed, opened up a world that had been vividly portrayed in her mind. The familiarity and sense of place and time returned.

Faith donned white cotton gloves in order to handle the most fragile manuscripts and photographs. She told Harry that she was conducting a genealogy search for ancestors, knowing that he would never understand her true purpose.

Little did Faith know that days would pass before she would find answers to her questions. She ambled into the library frustrated over their lack of progress. Maybe it was all a futile effort to try to recreate a past that never actually existed in reality, only in her head.

Harry met her with a sly twinkle in his gray eyes. A smile beamed on his drawn and wrinkled face and he had a skip in his step as he greeted her.

"You'll have to sit down for this one," he said, raking a hand through his thinning gray hair.

Faith trembled as she pulled out a chair and sat at the solid oak table. Bracing herself for shocking revelations, she met his gaze. "Let me have it."

"Miss Donahue, I've been doing a great deal of work on my own for you and have come up with some interesting results." He placed an overflowing folder of papers and photographs on the table.

Withdrawing a photograph from the folder, Harry handed it to her with a broad grin.

"Oh, Harry." Faith gasped as she took the photograph.

The sepia–toned photograph showed in exquisite detail a majestic Queen Anne Victorian with its turret, ornate trim, and front porch. She would have recognized the house anywhere. Flipping over the photograph, the words in fine script read, "92 Sacramento Street, Circa. 1908."

Each minute detail was vividly captured by the photographer's lens. From the front garden with flowering cherry trees to the porch furnished in fine wicker. The porch had wicker furnishings! When she saw it in 1906, it was bare. Confused, she closed her eyes trying to remember more about the house as it was versus the way it was now. Seeing the house was a good start, she realized, but didn't tell very much about its owners.

"Here's another one." Harry handed her another photograph.

She set down the photo of the house and reached for the next one. The photograph also featured the home's exterior but a man was standing in front of it. He was tall and dapper in a double–breasted suit with straight–cut trousers that accented his lithe frame. A bowler hat with a curled brim was set upon his head, a head was held high with regal elegance. His stance made her tremble. She squinted to decipher the features of his face.

There was no mistaking him.

"Doctor Ian Forrester," she muttered, heat enveloping her.

"Hey, you're right," Harry said. "Says so right on the back."

She turned over the photograph. "Doctor Ian Forrester" was written in flowery script.

"Oh, Harry." She looked up at him, tears misting her eyes. "You don't know what this means to me."

He was real. Doctor Ian Forrester really existed and he looked much the same as she remembered. This wasn't a head–injury–induced fantasy. This was real. She went back in time. She actually went back in time!

"There's more," Harry said with glee in his voice. He reached into the file and gingerly removed a crinkled, yellowed newspaper. "Better be careful with this one."

Faith carefully took the newspaper and set it down on the table. The ornate type revealed it to be the obituary page. She took a deep breath, grateful and yet fearful of what she might read.

Ian Andrew Forrester, M.D., Esteemed Physician, Husband, and Father

Seeing his name in newsprint made her heart pump faster, her body warm and shivering at the same time. Doctor Forrester was a real person who lived and died. She read the impressive first paragraph of his obituary, a biography chronicling the life of a well–educated and well–respected man. Yet, it hadn't captured the essence of the man she had known. His arrogance, humor, stubbornness, and deep love and devotion to his son were absent. Tears swelled in her eyes. He was dead. Somehow, she had managed to meet him when he was young and alive. She wondered why, of all the people who had resided in San Francisco during 1906, she had met him.

As she continued reading, one line glued her to her seat.

Survived by his wife, Faith Donahue Forrester, son Andrew James Forrester, and daughter Clarice Forrester Williams.

Faith Donahue Forrester? She was married to him? How? When she left, they had barely been on speaking terms.

"Oh my God!" Faith gasped loud enough for other patrons to turn around and stare at her in the quiet library. She covered her mouth with a shaking hand. Faith Donahue Forrester!

"If you think that's something, look at what else I found," Harry said, proud of his success. He handed her a yellowed photograph.

Faith took the photograph. Her eyes focused on it in total disbelief. It was a family portrait of the Forresters posed in front of 92 Sacramento Street. The husband was standing tall in his suit and bowler hat, the wife in a simple shirtwaist with a plumed hat perched on her head. Two young children stood in front of them. The little boy was a duplicate of his father. The little girl with the curly locks was barely out of diapers. Faith yearned to scream but put her knuckles in her mouth to suppress the urge.

"Your grandparents, huh?" Harry asked. "You're the spitting image of your grandmother."

Faith stared, eyes transfixed on the photograph. There was no denying it. The woman in the photograph was she. She was Mrs. Ian Forrester. She was the one Doctor Forrester held about the waist. Andrew was holding hands with his sister, her child. She had a child, the little girl she dreamed of and thought she'd never meet. The house was their house. Faith began to shake so badly she could hardly stay in her seat.

"Is something wrong?" Harry asked, concern wrinkling his brow.

"I…I'll be fine. I'm just shocked, that's all," Faith mumbled.

"It's against policy but I'll go get you some water anyway. I won't have you fainting on me." Harry said.

When he left, Faith stashed the family photograph in her deep jacket pocket, covering it with a tissue. So Harry wouldn't notice, she neatly rearranged his file of archival information and photographs.

She drew a deep breath and opened her notebook. She had enough information to continue her search if she so desired. There were burial plot numbers, names and addresses. After what she learned, she wondered if further research was necessary. There was no doubt in her mind. She had, indeed, traveled back through time.

With her discovery came more confusion. If her destiny was back in the San Francisco of 1906, what was she doing in the San Francisco of 2006?

CHAPTER 13

"SURE DOES LOOK LIKE YOU," Clarice said, comparing the woman in the photograph to Faith, seated at her side in her car.

"It is me."

"This is strange. I never would've believed you if I hadn't seen this, the writing on the back, and the photocopy of the obituary." Clarice shook her head.

"Well, do you believe me now?" Faith asked with a grin.

"It doesn't seem possible. The resemblance, though, is remarkable. The name is more than coincidental. The little girl even has my name." Her eyes met Faith's, bewildered and puzzled.

"That's why I want you to go with me to the cemetery today."

"You know how I don't like cemeteries." Clarice tapped the steering wheel with her long airbrushed nails.

"Look on the bright side, you aren't being buried there." Faith chuckled.

Clarice rolled her eyes and laughed. "I'll tell you, this has to be the strangest stuff I've ever heard of or seen. Now tell me, what are you gonna do when you see your name on the headstone? Have the body dug up?"

At the cemetery, they hiked over grassy knolls on a mission. Faith perused a plot map she obtained from the cemetery's office.

She and Clarice stepped over the modern, flat headstones, avoiding the old projecting ones in search of the Forrester family plot.

"Let's see, Row 2, Section 5," Faith said.

"After this, I think I'm gonna ask to be cremated," Clarice said, drawing her trench coat closed tight against her chest.

The breeze was kicking up and a misty chill filled the morning air. Fitting weather for a stroll through a deserted cemetery. Weekday mornings, between holidays, were quiet except for the occasional parade of limousines, hearses, and mourners.

"Aha!" Faith squealed upon sighting a granite monument of an angel with spread wings protecting the plot beneath. The inscription at the base was engraved FORRESTER.

Clarice moved to Faith's side. Faith pointed to the row of headstones and became somber, her bottom lip trembling as she read the names.

"Ian Andrew Forrester," Faith said. "He was eighty when he died."

Clarice set her hand on Faith's shoulder.

"Faith Donahue Forrester," Faith read, feeling nauseous. "She was seventy–five and died shortly after the doctor."

"Of a broken heart?"

Faith looked up, tears swelling in her eyes. "Clarice, I'm going to die at age seventy–five."

Clarice scoffed. "This is ridiculous. How do you know? That Faith died years ago. You're alive now, standing here with me."

"But, if I go back in time I'll live until age seventy–five. Can't you see?"

"This isn't making sense. Pretty soon I'll be losing it." Clarice turned away.

Faith reached out and grasped her by the shoulders. "Please, Clarice, I had to let you know about this. Someone has to know. When I vanish next time you'll know where I am and know that I'm safe and leading a long life."

Clarice spun around to face her. "You plan on disappearing again?"

"I don't know how or when. The obituary, the photograph, the headstone all seem to say that my destiny is back in 1906."

"It seems to say. Isn't there anyone who's alive who can settle this once and for all? You're relying on a bunch of old papers and stuff."

"Well." Faith turned toward the row of weathered headstones. "Our daughter died just fifteen years ago. If only I could have known her as a grown woman."

Faith drew a deep breath of misty air feeling sickened by all the death and grieving, all of the morbid thoughts filling her confused mind.

"Wait, there isn't a headstone for Andrew. I wonder what happened to Andrew."

Clarice grabbed her arm. "Oh, please. Let's get out of here. This situation is getting creepier by the minute."

Harry at the library had dug up information on another survivor. Andrew Forrester was still alive. Though partially deaf and blind, he had lived independently until about ten years ago when a hip fracture sent him to the nursing home.

Hospitality Home was nestled in the suburban environment of commercial businesses and restaurants outside of Oakland. Surrounded by the living, the home was inhabited by those closer to dying. Faith viewed nursing homes as a sort of purgatory for those hovering between life and death. Though Hospitality Home was lovely and well–managed, and neither reeked of urine nor had patients strapped in wheelchairs, the mood was still depressing.

Faith strolled past rooms of patients lying in near vegetative states, those whose bodies were gone but memories were alive, and those with neither body nor memory. The home's supervisor had been hesitant in letting Faith visit. She wasn't a relative of a patient but because of Andrew's advanced age and alert mind, she thought no harm could be done. Faith said she was an old friend.

How could she explain that she was his step-mother? The elderly needed all the friends they could get.

A nurse led Faith down the shiny, checkered–tile corridor, Faith's heels the only sound in the empty hall. The nurse pointed to a room with a half–open door and smiled

Faith could see a figure slumped in a wheelchair, his form silhouetted against the bright sunlight streaming through the window. As the nurse rapped on the door, the figure sat up, startled, his head turning to face the door. A chill ran up her spine as Faith gazed at the elderly man who was really her stepson, as preposterous as it now seemed. She had left him as a sweet young boy with a blanket and stuffed bear.

"Doctor Forrester, you have a visitor," the nurse announced.

Doctor? Andrew had apparently followed in his father's footsteps. A lump formed in her throat.

As Faith entered the room, the elderly man squinted to get a closer look. Though the hair was cottony white, the face parched and wrinkled, the eyes still sparkled with mischief. Faith's gaze locked on to his, tears forming in the corner of her eyes.

"Mom? You look like my mother," he said in an aged, raspy voice.

"Andrew, you remember me?" Faith asked, a trembling smile on her lips.

"Faith…Faith." Andrew reached up his frail arms.

The nurse pushed a wooden chair next to the wheelchair and motioned for Faith to sit. The nurse nodded and left the room. Faith grabbed Andrew's withered hand and held it clasped in hers. She closed her eyes for a moment to regain her composure as the emotions of lost time swelled within her. The warmth of his hand felt comforting and reassuring. Andrew was real and alive.

"I…I always believed you. Now I know, now I know. After all these years I finally know." Andrew stared at her. "Look at you, as pretty as when we met, and how long has it been?"

"You know?"

"Oh, yes. I knew there was something special about you when

you vanished in front of Dad and me after the earthquake. I later found your things that Dad and you had hidden away. The family secret"

Faith squeezed his hand. "It's so good to see you. Now I know for sure that all of it was real. I'm not crazy. I did go back in time."

"And you must go back again. You must," Andrew urged, a fire of determination glowing in her eyes.

"Andrew, there's so much I don't understand." Releasing his hand, Faith reached in her pocket and pulled out the yellowed family photograph. She showed it to him

He eyed the portrait, a smile radiating from his face. "Our loving family."

"Is it me? Am I really the woman married to Ian Forrester?"

He nodded. "Yes, of course, that's why you must return."

"I don't understand why your father would marry me. He was in love with Miss LaDue?"

"Miss La Doo-doo," Andrew snickered. "You have to go back so that he doesn't marry her. I always hated her. In time, you and Dad will discover that only by being together will you find the happiness you both so desperately seek." He returned the photo to Faith.

Faith looked at the photograph. "I find it all so difficult to comprehend."

"Just go back and you will see how love can transcend time itself."

"How?"

"What fun would life be if we knew all the answers?"

With age came wisdom. Faith reached out and hugged the frail man, feeling more bones than flesh. Releasing him Faith looked into Andrew's eyes. "Has life been good to you?"

"I've lived this long, haven't I?"

Faith smiled. "I'm glad that you have."

"Married once myself and fathered some wonderful children. I'm not telling you about them or my wife now. You'll just have to go back and find out for yourself." He winked.

"Andrew, you were a sinister little boy and now a sinister man."

He laughed. "Think I'd change?"

Faith shook her head.

"Will you promise me something?" Andrew's tone became low and serious.

"What?"

"When you go back, don't tell me my future. I want to live life day by day. Please promise me."

"I promise." Faith took his hand and squeezed it.

"I'm getting old and tired. I can't go back. Wouldn't want to. Lived long enough already." He sighed. "So glad to see your face. I can now die in peace knowing what I believed all along was true."

"Don't talk about dying. We've just been reunited."

"No, we'll be reunited when you go back. You will go back. You must. My life depends on it."

CHAPTER 14

"*F*AITH, FAITH!" HIS VOICE RANG *out amidst the whirlpool of people gathered in Lafayette Park. Attired in various stages of dress and undress the men, women, and children were reaching up to him. Faces contorted with anguish were begging for help. Fingers grasped at his tweed suit, clawing at the fabric.*

"Come back, Faith! I need you!" Doctor Forrester cried out, eyes darting through the crowd in search of one who could not be found.

A dense fog crept up from beneath his feet, enveloping his legs, his chest, his neck, until his face vanished within its thickness. The crowd disappeared with him.

Out of the fog came a whimper, "Miss Donahue, where are you? I miss you! I miss you!"

Andrew's tearful voice choked out the words, his face unseen, hidden in the murky fog. The fog turned from gray to black until there was nothing left but darkness and the echo of voices, far away voices.

The voices shattered the stillness of the night. Faith jumped up in her bed, shaking. Her nightgown was damp with cold perspiration. She had the urge to answer the distant voices, to call and assure them. The silence of her bedroom made her realize that it was just a strange dream. If not for the library research, the visit to the cemetery, and the conversation with Andrew, she would have thought herself crazy. She reached over to flip on the bedside lamp. In the light she saw the framed photograph of the family who stood lovingly close. She touched her finger to the woman who was the spitting image of herself and to the man who had his arm about her waist, Dr. and Mrs. Ian Forrester.

"How can I come back to you when I'm a hundred years in the future? I don't know how," she wondered aloud, haunted by the photograph and the memories.

She lay back against her pillows, holding the framed photograph in front of her. How do I go back? The idea of returning to 1906 seemed impossible. She shook her head, hoping that the thought would somehow fall away like cobwebs being brushed aside. Instead, the desire to go back grew stronger in her mind.

She could envision herself in the San Francisco of 1906 building a new life out of the rubble of her old life. Whether she was in 1906 or 2006, she would be starting over. Her marriage was over. Years of mistakes, misconceptions, of assumptions, and broken dreams could not be relived. The San Francisco of 2006 held no real future for her, only reminders of what was and what could have been.

"Just go back and you will see how love can transcend time itself." Andrew's words rang in her mind.

Love? She sighed. After all the hell Brad put her through, how could she ever trust a man again? How could she ever love again? She couldn't allow herself to become that vulnerable again. The sickness called love was something she needed to avoid.

As she looked at the photograph, the image smiling back at her made her tingle. Serene contentment radiated from her face. The glowing eyes, the secure, comfortable stance. Doctor Forrester's hand grasped her waist as they stood intimately close. His eyes beamed at the camera, his happiness evident in his tilted head and confident pose. Little

Andrew held the hand of a little girl, a duplicate of Faith herself. A little girl. Faith had always dreamed of having a little girl. As she had grown older, she had given up the hope of ever having a child. In going back, she would have the opportunity to have the family she had so longed for.

She leaned over and set the photograph on the nightstand, face–down, and turned out the light. The whole scenario seemed like some warped dream or fairy tale. Falling in love with the doctor, marrying him, having sex with him, bearing his child seemed ridiculous. When she left she was merely Andrew's nanny, and even that role was tenuous. The doctor was arrogant and had shown minimal interest in her. He was about to fire her for mental instability. She wasn't even his friend yet alone the love of his life.

Closing her eyes, she thought of him. Doctor Ian Forrester seemed more like a creation from Emily Bronte in his handsome, dark, brooding way. His towering height and lean dashing form cut quite a figure. He exuded that subtle, natural sexuality that most women found attractive. Unlike Brad he wasn't the yuppie type. He was a real man. For that she was grateful. Thoughts of how he would perform in bed invaded her mind. His hands were soft, his fingers slender and gentle. His lips were full, his body well–proportioned. She squirmed under the covers. This was getting out of hand.

If the opportunity to begin a new life were possible, if Doctor Forrester would fall in love with and marry her, would she take a chance and go back? How could she go back? What risks were involved? The chance of winning the lottery was probably better than the odds of her returning to 1906 San Francisco.

She pieced together the events leading to her original time travel episode. Every little detail. From the automobile careening off the cliff to her surfacing in the cold, placid waters of the bay came back. An idea struck so suddenly it was like a light bulb flashing on in her mind.

"That's it!" she screamed. "There's only one way I can go back."

She smiled while she lay in the dark formulating her plan. The plan would call for recreating the same scene as the last time. It would call for a red Jaguar automobile, the cliff side parking space overlooking the bay, a clear starry night, and would have to take place at the exact month, day, and time. There would be no guarantee of success, she realized. Failure would mean certain death.

"For all intents and purposes, I'm dead anyway." She sighed.

She would have one year to get her present affairs in order and to plan for the riskiest journey of her life. Much work needed to be done, so many loose ends to tie up.

Her life in 2006 would have to be closed out completely.

Faith couldn't explain the urgency she felt but the idea seemed so right. Nothing had ever seemed so right in her life, as if some invisible force was leading her on this journey.

In one year, she intended to be back in the San Francisco of 1906.

CHAPTER 15

FAITH COUNTED THE DAYS WHILE closing out her life in 2006. The Forrester family photograph and thoughts of Andrew heightened her anticipation of beginning a new life in 1906. She kept her final plan a secret, as secure as the sterling in Doctor Forrester's parlor safe. Even Clarice's questions and concerns failed to deter her. Faith would fulfill what she perceived as her destiny regardless of the consequences.

Bradley Clark Donahue III was to be released from jail and exonerated from the charge of attempted murder against his wife. The evidence of clutch tampering could not be linked to him. Without Faith's testimony and the fact that he had taken out a million–dollar life insurance policy, with a double–indemnity clause, for himself as well, he could no longer be held. As for his mob connections, they could not be proven. Sergeant Schmidt couldn't understand Faith's change of heart and willingness to set Brad free.

"Thanks, Faith," Brad said, tapping her on the shoulder as she walked from the civic center.

Faith stopped walking and turned to meet his gaze.

"What made you change your mind?" he asked.

"I don't want to hold grudges. Even you're entitled to a life," she answered without emotion.

"So, I guess the next time we'll meet is in divorce court?"

"Not necessarily."

Brad stepped back, startled. "What? What are you saying?"

"I'm not contesting the divorce," she said, her gaze unwavering. He was squirming in his Gucci loafers.

"You're not?"

"No."

"Yo!" Brad took another step back. "What's going on? I don't get it. Where's the catch?"

"No catch." She sighed. There was a time when she would have had him nailed in court, his name and reputation dragged in the mud, and his pockets and bank accounts emptied. It's what he deserved for using her and deceiving her. Where she was going, though, his alimony payments couldn't be mailed.

"What is it you want?" he asked, raking his hair back with his fingers.

"The house on Sacramento Street, for starters."

"The house, huh?"

"Yes. I don't want your little Twinkie living in my house."

He scoffed. "That house is too old for Pam's taste anyway."

"I know. She's still into Barbie's Dream Home."

"Faith?" He stepped forward, pointing a finger at her with a scowl on his face.

She stood firm, maintaining her steady gaze. "I also want one million cash."

"You want what?"

"Come off it, Brad. We both know you're worth well over four million dollars."

"I—"

"I'll have my attorney contact yours about setting up an appointment to get the paperwork finalized," Faith said, turning her back to him and walking forward.

"Faith?" he called.

She stopped and pivoted to face him.

"What do you plan on doing with your life?"

Did he really care?

She smiled. "I plan on going back to a simpler place and time."

"I…I want you to know that I didn't want to hurt you. I

didn't rig your car and, well, with Pam things just happened." He shrugged his shoulders. For a brief moment he looked like the college preppie she met and fell in love with. Appearances were deceiving with Brad. One look in his eyes revealed a hardened soul. If only she had looked deeper into his eyes when she was young. Too old too soon, too smart too late, her mother used to say.

"You were never honest with me," she said.

"No. I wasn't honest. I was afraid."

"Not of me, but of losing all your money, your lifestyle, right Brad?"

He flinched. "Divorces can get nasty."

"I'm saving you that."

"I don't get it."

"Maybe one day you will."

They met with their attorneys, worked out a settlement, and dissolved their marriage. Faith's attorney couldn't understand her resolve in not contesting the divorce and fighting for alimony. Where she was going she didn't need much. For a woman who had grown accustomed to luxury and modern convenience, she realized that the most important things in life could not be bought or invented. A faithful and loving husband, children, true friends, health, a happy home, and a long life were more important than microwaves and Jaguars.

The house at 92 Sacramento Street was titled to Faith free and clear and one million dollars placed in her savings account. Brad practically danced on air, whistling, as he left the attorney's office. Faith smirked. She wasn't completely done with him yet. First things first.

Faith's first goal was to transform her elegant Victorian home into an historical masterpiece. She hired a renowned restoration architect and, together with an interior designer, they outlined a design scheme for the home. Relying on memory, Faith's goal was to return the house to its original 1906 grandeur.

All contemporary accoutrements, from the laminate kitchen cabinets to the tinted china bathroom fixtures were ripped out. Wooden floors were sanded and refinished, molding stripped and stained, windows and doors replaced to reflect a turn–of–the–century mood.

Faith scrounged antique shops, auction houses, catalogues, and showrooms, selecting period–appropriate wall coverings, rugs, furniture, and accessories to reflect the time period. Gas lamp fixtures were hung, draperies created, rugs, furniture, and plants placed.

Months passed before she was able to walk through the result. Faith basked in the transformation. Parquet floors glistened, scattered with Persian and Tabriz rugs. Worn leather scented the library, lemon wax the parlor. The restoration was complete down to the marble–topped parlor safe in the corner of the dining room. She half–expected Andrew to come bounding in at any moment.

The first night she slept in the restored bedroom, she sensed renewal and contentment. There was comfort in the flannel granny gown and the downy feather bed. In the moonlight she scanned the outline of the baked–on enamel iron footboard, the towering rosewood wardrobe, and the commode complete with porcelain toilet set. Her house had become a home. Memories of her awakening in the same room in 1906 flooded her mind. Pleasant memories. Soon, if all her plans worked, she would be back there, back in time. She knew where she belonged.

Three more days. Everything was on schedule. Faith dressed accordingly for her noon appointment. The prim powder blue Chanel suit was appropriate for a meeting with the stoic San Francisco Historic Preservation Society. They were in for quite a surprise.

"So," Faith announced at the meeting, "I am donating my re-stored home, one of the few original survivors of the 1906 earth-quake and fire, to your historic preservation society. It is my desire that this home serve as a museum and a reminder of simpler times now past. The home is the legacy of Doctor Ian Forrester, who lovingly built it and resided within it. I want future generations to treasure this fine example of Victorian architecture. To secure its future, I have established The Forrester Trust to finance main-tenance and future repairs."

The board gasped, taken aback by Faith's generous offer. Most homeowners chose profit over generosity. Fine historical prop-erties were rare and commanded high prices in a competitive market like San Francisco. Pacific Heights had some of the most expensive and priceless real estate in the city. Donated homes were scarce and usually came from eccentric dowagers not pert young women.

"Are you certain?" the board president asked, peering over the reading glasses perched on her nose.

"Yes," Faith replied with a contented grin, more certain of her decision than those seated at the conference table realized. She was preserving her past for the future.

After the meeting, her attorney met with theirs to process the paperwork and finalize the deal. When the deal was complete, her attorney drew her aside.

Cyrus Jones was one of the sharpest legal minds in San Fran-cisco. Towering and hulky in stature, he cut quite a dramatic presence in the courtroom. Only his Coke–bottle reading glasses hinted at the brains behind the brawn. Faith trusted him implic-itly. Not only was he Clarice's big brother but a man of integrity and honesty.

"Faith, what's going on?" he asked in his soft, self–assured voice. "I don't get it. You sell yourself short to Brad and now you donate your home and the remainder of your settlement."

She smiled. "Don't worry about me. I know what I'm doing."

"Clarice said you resigned from the school. Where are you going to live? What are you going to live on? We're worried about you."

"I have a plan. Trust me," she said with a firm voice.

"I want to. I really do. I've known you for years. You've always been so rational, until now."

"I've never been so confident, so free. I've been given a new lease on life."

CHAPTER 16

BRADLEY CLARK DONAHUE III ALWAYS parked his shiny red Jaguar in the same reserved parking space in the parking garage next to his Van Ness Avenue office building. The car was his pride and joy, a sign of his success and an extension of his ego. Faith knew this. She also knew that it was identical to the car she had owned, the one that ended up in San Francisco Bay. She had a set of keys to Brad's beloved car, since she always kept an extra set of his in case of emergency, and conveniently neglected to return the keys upon finalization of their divorce. The car was an important part of her plan.

Tuesday evening was Brad's late work night. Faith knew that Brad was a stickler for routine and a man of habit, a time management guru. The timing couldn't have been much better.

Faith rode the trolley to a stop near Brad's parking garage. Entering the garage's elevator, she pushed a button for the second level. A nervous exhilaration swept over her as she exited the elevator. His car was easy to spot with its glistening candy apple red finish. She removed her set of keys from her shirt pocket and beeped off the car alarm with the key chain. Grateful that it was still programmed the same way, she walked up to the sleek car, unlocked the car door, tossed her duffle bag and backpack in the back seat, and slid into the supple leather driver's seat. As she placed the key in the ignition she smiled. The car was identical to hers down to the color-coordinated coffee cup on the dash. Brad's creed of "two of everything" was paying off. Even his

Pam gave him twins, identical boys, recently. Faith sighed. After overcoming this hurdle, she was confident of the success of her evening's plan.

She checked her wristwatch. In an hour she was meeting Clarice at the cliff side restaurant, the same place they met that fateful night when she became a time traveler.

After taking a deep breath, she released the clutch and shifted in reverse. The car was a smooth piece of precision engineering. Too bad it was going to end up on the bottom of the bay.

Before meeting Clarice, Faith stopped by the house at 92 Sacramento Street for a last look. Withdrawing the brass key from under the front door mat, she entered her home for the last time in 2007. The next time she hoped to enter the home would be 100 years in the past. She walked through the parquet foyer and up the stairs, stroking the smooth sloping curves of the mahogany banister. She closed her eyes for a moment wondering if she was crazy or, indeed, the recipient of a special miracle. Tonight she would find out.

After touring her home, room-by-room, she walked to the front door. Satisfied that it was in caring hands, a part of history to be preserved and treasured, she exited through the front door and locked the brass latch for a final time. She was closing the door on her past. Closing the door on one life.

Before driving away, she glanced back at the grand Queen Ann Victorian with its turret, ornate trim, and sprawling front porch.

"'Til we meet again," she whispered, as the reflection of the home grew smaller in the rearview mirror.

The parking place was reserved for her. The maitre d' had honored her request and she slipped the Jaguar in her cliff side space. As she peered out the front window, dusk was descending over the city. An eerie shiver ran up and down her spine. The water below seemed so dark, so deep, and so ominous. She swallowed hard assuring herself that tonight was her only hope for a future, a future that lay in the past.

Clarice was already seated at the corner table when Faith strode in. Candlelight flickered from a single taper, casting a golden glow on her caramel skin and a sparkle to her ebony eyes. Faith gazed at her best friend knowing that this would be their last meeting. She wanted to freeze this moment in her memory. A lump formed in her throat. Clarice had always been there to listen, to encourage, and to hold her hand. Leaving her best friend was the most difficult part of this final plan.

As Faith took her seat, Clarice held up her glass of Chablis as if in a toast.

"You need a drink, my friend. You're so pale and sullen. You look like you've seen a ghost," Clarice said.

Faith realized that she had been staring like a spaced–out zombie. She forced a smile and blinked back tears.

Clarice waved down a nearby waiter and when he approached said, "Get this girl a Chardonnay. Pronto."

"Yes, ma'am," he replied, rushing off.

"I'm worried about you, Faith." Clarice set down her glass of wine, clasping her hands on the table.

"No need. Everything's taken care of."

"That's what I mean. I have a mind to lock you up in a room and throw away the key. I don't want you going off and doing something irrational."

"Just because I've been a bit frazzled, doesn't mean…"

"Faith, we've been friends long enough. You can't fool me. I know that losing Brad has been difficult but it's not bad enough to give up your life for." Clarice's eyes could have burned a hole through her.

"What are you implying?"

"First, you refuse to fight Brad in court, accepting a pittance of a settlement. You spend all of it on a home you donate to charity. You quit your job. You have no savings or income. You gave away your belongings. What am I to think?"

Faith smiled. "That I'm going on a long journey."

The waiter arrived, setting down Faith's wine. When he left, she lifted the glass.

"Congratulate me, Clarice. I'm going back to begin a new life, to fulfill my destiny."

"Your destiny is not to kill yourself. I won't let you do it."

Faith tossed back her head in laughter.

"You think that I'm going to commit suicide?"

"Sure looks that way. Nothing that life hands out is bad enough to end it all."

Faith sipped her wine and set down the glass.

"Clarice, after all I've confided in you? You still don't understand?"

"What? You mean all this talk about going back in time to some hunk of a doctor in 1906?" She scoffed.

"You saw the photograph, the headstone, the obituary. I told you about Andrew. How can you doubt me? I'm going back."

Clarice threw up her hands, her bangle bracelets rattling. "That's impossible! Time travel is pure science fiction. Fiction is not reality."

"You saw the proof." Faith took another sip of wine.

"We see what we want to see. The mind and the eyes can play tricks." Clarice set her hands, tightened into fists, on the table.

"Clarice you must understand. I want you to understand."

She shook her head of jet curls. "I want to understand. I really do. It's just so...so preposterous."

"If only I could take you back with me. But you have your destiny here, with Reggie and the children." She reached out across the table to take Clarice's hand.

Clarice unclenched her fingers and held on.

"Please, don't get morbid on me."

"Clarice, you're my best friend, the closest to a family that I have left. I'm going to miss you, really miss you."

Their eyes locked, both choking back tears.

"I just wanted to spend this evening to celebrate our friendship. I want you to know that someday I will be back. I don't want you to be surprised," Faith assured.

"After all that's gone on lately, nothing will surprise me about you."

"I'm going to be happy, really happy." Faith let tears escape from her eyes.

"I hope so," Clarice reached up to dab her eyes that were getting damp and misty. She cleared her throat. "So tell me, how do you plan on accomplishing this feat?"

"I can't say," Faith said. "I can't risk anything going wrong."

"Like me stopping you?"

"You'll find out, Clarice. I'll leave a sign. You'll know."

The waiter came to take their orders.

"I don't know about you, Clarice, but I'm starving. I'll need all my strength for the journey ahead."

After seeing a reluctant Clarice off, Faith retrieved her duffle bag from the car and went into the ladies' restroom. She withdrew her finds from a vintage clothing store and began her transformation. The white starched shirtwaist with the high stiff collar edged in lace was adorned with a cameo she found in a display case. The black taffeta skirt reached the ankles of her new retro black leather lace–up boots. She looked very much the proper Victorian lady. She chuckled, though, for she refused to purchase a stayed corset and black wool stockings, preferring Victoria's Secret and Lycra tights.

Satisfied with the chignon she pinned atop her head accented with a tortoiseshell comb, she sashayed out of the restroom and through the restaurant to stares and whispers.

Outside, she threw her bag of modern clothes in the dumpster.

Entering her car, she removed an oversized, overstuffed waterproof backpack from the back seat and struggled into it. She knew it had to have been the silliest idea yet. She just wanted to take back some of the contrivances of the modern world. She had selected carefully and yet the bag still bulged. She just hoped that the backpack wouldn't hamper her return or drag her down into the depths of the bay. As it was, even with the seat pushed back as far as possible, sitting was cramped.

She wasn't as nervous as she thought she'd be. Thoughts of turning back and changing her mind were not a possibility. She had planned too long and too carefully to give up. The whole idea of going back in time may have seemed an impossible gamble but she determined that it was all or nothing. Either she would end up back in 1906 or dead. Either way she would be removed from a life and a world she no longer knew or fit.

CHAPTER 17

FAITH AWAKENED SHIVERING SO VIOLENTLY that her teeth chattered. She opened her eyes, squinting as she adjusted to the darkness enveloping her. Misty fog blanketed her in thick, cold foreboding. She drew a breath tasting salt and a musty dank. For a moment she wondered if she was dead or alive.

Moving ever so gingerly, she rolled over on her side. Her arms brushed against something slick and slippery, dew kissed grass. Propping herself up on stiff arms, she lifted her head. As she looked up, a patch of fog cleared revealing a black velvet sky littered with stars sparkling like faceted diamonds. Their beauty and the tranquil silence made her wonder if this could be heaven.

A horse's neighing and distant voices startled her from her thoughts. She sat up, her heart beginning to palpitate. Did she survive the trip back in time? Was it 1906? 1907? She tried to rise to her feet but felt burdened and held back. She than realized that she was still carrying the backpack. The backpack!

With new–found strength she crawled up to her feet and began to stagger toward the voices that grew louder at every step. Through the fog, men, women, children, the old, the young, rich, and poor swarmed the park like refugees just off a boat at Ellis Island. Some sat on the ground while others stood huddled amidst a hodgepodge of belongings, barking dogs, squawking caged birds, screaming babies, and raging bonfires. Some were bruised, others bandaged, a few shell–shocked. None seemed to notice her. All seemed lost in distant thoughts or distracted by the moment. She walked amongst them, another displaced and confused person.

She had to get answers. She had to know. Had she returned?

Approaching an elderly man who sat hunched, fanning a fire, she asked, "What day is this?"

He looked up, his beard as grizzled as his face. "April 21, me thinks."

"What year?"

"1906."

She smiled, wanting to scream out. Yes! Yes! She did it! She made it back!

"Thank you," she said to the man who returned to his fire, unfazed by her strange questions.

She moved on with a spring in her step. She wanted to laugh but for the grim reality around her. Misery surrounded her in hollow eyes, pursed lips, cries of anguish, and tears. People in various states of dress and undress, dirty, holding on to all their worldly possessions, reduced to what they could wear or carry. Acrid smoke lingered in the air. So, this was the aftermath of the earthquake and fire. These were the citizens of San Francisco who were routed from their homes, escaping with their lives. As she approached the top of the hill in the park, she could see the smoldering ruins of the city. Gutted buildings were silhouetted against a backdrop of crimson flames that still raged out of control. The sound of crackling wood, the pops of ignited dynamite blended with voices. She felt like Scarlet O'Hara in *Gone With The Wind* who stood watching Atlanta burn. Faith watched San Francisco burn. It was no wonder that everyone called it the

Great Fire of 1906 instead of the Great Earthquake. The earth may have shaken but the fire is what consumed the city. Like a phoenix, she knew it would rise from the ashes, triumphant. She knew, but the lost souls surrounding her would have to find out.

The walk to Sacramento Street was exhausting and fraught with danger. From the crumbling buildings and smoldering debris to gun–toting police with a curfew and orders to shoot to kill, Faith somehow made it.

The house at 92 Sacramento Street stood just as she remembered it, stately and unblemished. She opened the picket gate and ambled up the brick path. A queasy, dizzy feeling overcame her as she stumbled up the front steps. The porch's floorboards creaked at her every step. Lugging the heavy backpack up and down the hilly streets, the nauseating scent of burnt wood and flesh, the dank and heat was taking its toll. She felt clammy, shaky, and yet happy. She knew that this was where she was meant to be.

She reached for the brass lion's head doorknocker and rapped. When there was no answer, she rapped again.

The heavy door creaked open and Bridget stood filling the doorway. Her eyes popped open and her mouth gaped as she screamed out in startled awe.

"Miss Donahue!"

"Bridget," Faith managed to say before collapsing in a heap on the parquet foyer floor.

The scene seemed oddly familiar. Faith awakened nestled in the cushy featherbed. Rubbing her eyes open, she saw the white enamel iron footboard, the tall rosewood wardrobe, dresser, chiffonier, and the commode set for her toilette. The gilt–framed mirror hung above the mantel while a fire glowed in the hearth. Tapestry draperies covered the windows and a wicker chair was set in the corner.

Faith gasped as she gazed at the chair. Slouched in it was a dozing Doctor Forrester. His head lay back against the backrest, his arms folded on his lap, and his long legs stretched out in front.

At the sound of her voice, his eyes darted open and he jumped up, startled, from the seat. He met her gaze with eyes wide open. He brushed at the wrinkles in his dark trousers and the cotton shirt, unfastened at the neck. Unshaven with tousled hair, he looked so different from the impeccable, poised man she remembered. He appeared younger, more approachable, more vulnerable. He stepped toward the bed with hesitation.

She stared at him, perplexed over his manner and behavior. He was handsome in a brooding, almost wild, way. She drew the quilt up to her neck as she scooted up in the bed.

"So we meet again, Doctor Forrester," Faith said in a near whisper. As she peered into his dark eyes, she couldn't help but think about the photograph and their destiny. She trembled, gripping at the quilt until her fingers felt numb.

"Who are you?" he asked, his eyes boring down at her as he stood beside the bed.

"Faith Donahue."

"Who are you, really?"

"I told you."

He shook his head. "Perhaps, I'm asking the wrong question. What are you?" he asked, his eyes with the flickering gold intensity of the hearth's fire.

"I don't understand."

"What kind of being are you?"

"The human kind, I can assure you." Her lips trembled as she tried to smile.

"I do not know of any human who can predict earthquakes and fires, who can vanish into thin air, who possesses strange objects...need I go on?" He smoothed back his hair with splayed fingers.

"A human, who through some quirk of nature and fate, has traveled back and forth through time," she explained in an even, steady tone. She had to make him believe her.

He sighed. "So you have said before. It just isn't possible."

"But yet I'm here. I returned here."

He pounded his fist on the iron footboard. "Why? Why here? Why now? Why in my life?"

He knelt down at her bedside, his eyes level with hers. "I was a reasonable man before you came. Now I don't know what I am."

"Destiny."

"Destiny?"

She shrugged. "I have no other explanation."

"Destiny?"

"Believe me, no one was more surprised than me, to end up here in 1906. Yet, as I've discovered, it's where I belong. It's my destiny."

He stood. "I don't understand. I shall never understand."

"You're a learned man but no one has the answers to all the mysteries in life. Leave them to God."

He stared at her, puzzled.

"You forewarned us about the earthquake and fire. That much is certain. Our belongings were spared and we've had enough food and water stored up to be comfortable. Others are not so fortunate."

"I know. I saw them in Triangle Park when I returned."

He began to pace the floor as he spoke. "Since the cataclysm I have been out doctoring those in need, an overwhelming task. I came home for additional supplies only to hear Bridget screaming hysterically about your return. You were prone on my foyer floor, a heavy sack tied to your back. I have seen many a strange sight, but you were one to behold." He paused, turned toward her and took a deep breath. "You believe in adding drama to your comings and goings, don't you? The way you vanished before Andrew and I was quite remarkable. If not for my son and other witnesses, I would have thought it a trick of my imagination."

She interrupted. "I somehow was sent back to 2006 where I was found on the street with a gash on my head. It was considered strange that I would appear on a major thoroughfare wearing 1900's garb and babbling about the Great Earthquake."

"I still don't understand this talk about 2006." He pointed his finger at her.

"I can explain. If you would retrieve my backpack, I'll show you some of the things I brought back."

"You make it sound as if you were away on some holiday."

She snickered, curling her lip. "In a way, I was. Just bring me my pack...unless, of course, you already examined the contents?"

"The pack, as you call that monstrous bag, has not been touched. In this house we have viewed it as a Pandora's Box."

"I can assure you it doesn't contain snakes or plagues."

He walked over to the rosewood wardrobe. Opening a narrow door, he reached down and retrieved her heavy nylon backpack. Carrying it by the straps, he deposited it at her side on the bed. The bag sunk into the feather mattress. He pulled up the wicker chair and sat, analyzing her every move.

Faith glanced up at the doctor and down at the pack. She was inwardly amused at his interest and fear. He seemed genuinely concerned about the contents of her pack. In an era of tiny reticules and bulky steamer trunks, the nylon backpack had to be an unusual sight. The fabric nylon had yet to be invented and zippers were rather new.

As she unzipped the perimeter of the bag, Doctor Forrester sat back as if in fear of the contents leaping out at him. Faith smiled as the tightly packed contents began to pop out.

Doctor Forrester jumped in his seat, startled as three padded bras landed on the bed before him. Faith watched his face turn crimson as he stared at the leopard print and black lace one. Corsets never looked like that, she surmised.

Beneath her "unmentionables," Lycra tights and pantyhose, a cosmetics bag, were books, she reached in and withdrew a book on San Francisco. The heavy, oversized volume featured a color photograph of the Golden Gate Bridge on its cover. Like a child presenting "Show and Tell," she held up the book as if displaying it. The doctor stared at it, stroking his chin in contemplative silence.

"This is a book chronicling the history of San Francisco from the Gold Rush up until 2006," she explained. "On the cover is a color photograph of the famous Golden Gate Bridge, built in 1937."

"Impossible," he murmured.

She smiled, opening the book. Turning to the copyright page, she pointed out the year. "This book was published in early, 2006."

He squinted, leaning forward to read the fine print.

"Here." She snapped the book shut and handed it to him. "Look through its pages to catch a glimpse of the future. Just promise me one thing."

"What's that?" he asked as he gingerly accepted the book.

"That no one else be shown this book or told about me. The book and my past have to remain our secret."

"Are you afraid someone might have you committed?"

"Or display me in a circus sideshow?" She sighed. "Doctor, we can't chance altering any part of history, good or bad, just because of my arrival."

He shook his head, staring down at the book and up at her.

"Doctor, do you promise?"

He met her gaze. "I'm a man of my word."

"Promise?"

"Promise."

For a moment she thought time stood still as their eyes melded together. She wondered if the promise spoken was the same as the promise implied. She focused on him as he opened the book to the first page. Before him was a printed timeline of major events in the history of the world as well as in the city. His hands trembled as he fingered the words.

"Airplanes? A Titanic ship? World War? Women voting? Negroes as equals?

Man on the moon? This...these things are not possible. It cannot be. The early history is accurate but the future predictions... oh my." He looked up from the book, beads of perspiration forming on his brow.

"They are not predictions but fact. Those things will happen." She met his gaze, steady and assured. At least he was questioning and not arguing.

He shook his head as he turned the pages. He didn't want to believe what he saw and read. The photographs were all too real and the steady stream of inventions and transformations began to make some sense. Everything, though, was so far removed from the world as he knew it. Was there nothing left untouched? Would the world really be turned upside down and inside out as revealed in the thick volume?

"Everything is so complex," he muttered, unfolding the centerfold, revealing the city skyline in its 2006 glory. Buildings he couldn't recognize gleamed from the pages, the Transamerica Pyramid looming like a sentinel amidst the shiny skyscrapers.

"Life is very complex."

Faith sat up in the bed, bringing her knees up to her chest, hugging the covers against her. She felt more at ease, confident that he finally believed her. The book and its contents mesmerized him and she was assured that showing it to him was a smart move.

"I have never seen anything like this. It is like reading Nostradamus. The photographs, though, are so clear, magical, so real." He gazed at her. "Where did you get this book?"

"Don't worry. You can't buy it now. It won't be published for another hundred years."

He looked inside the dust jacket flap. "$29.95? For a book"

"Not a great sum in 2006."

"2006? Hmm." He shut the book and set it on the bed.

"Well, do you believe me now?" she asked.

"I'm so confused I don't know what to believe," he admitted. He glanced at her open backpack. "What else do you have in your bag of tricks?"

"More personal items." She pointed to the leopard bra that still lay in plain view.

He looked away. She could have sworn he was blushing.

"I brought you a gift," she said.

He looked at her, snickering. "A crystal ball?"

She removed a *Merck Manual* from her pack and handed the heavy volume to him.

"Another book?" he asked, accepting the thick book with the navy blue cover.

"Not just any book but a famous medical diagnostics book.

Some bedtime reading for you."

He set the book on his lap, keeping it closed.

"Aren't you at least going to open it?'

"Not now. I've had enough surprises for one day."

She knew that the biggest surprises were yet to come and he hadn't realized it yet.

CHAPTER 18

EVER SINCE FAITH DONAHUE VANISHED in mid–air and reappeared on his doorstep, Ian Forester had a difficult time doing anything but thinking about her and her unbelievable story. She was the most beguiling creature he had ever met. After having shown him the magical book on the futuristic San Francisco and a medical text that defied description, he didn't know what to make of her. She claimed to be a product of the future. There was no logical explanation for the strange artifacts she brought back, for the unusual articles of clothing and cosmetics, or for the confidence and independence she possessed. Faith was so different from other women, her manner and intellect far more progressive. He wished Miss LaDue were more like her. Her actions were so much more self–assured and liberated. He found her openness refreshing and her mind a challenge. She was unique but he couldn't bring himself to believe that she was a time traveler.

Time travelers were a thing of fiction.

He had to get to the bottom of her mystery. The scientist in him was running out of theories. She wasn't insane according to the medical texts. Her accounting of her life hadn't varied. Faith was unwavering in her story. The fact that she vanished in thin air defied all scientific explanation. The contents of her bulky bag defied description.

Perhaps more conversation would unravel the mystery. He was a man who thrived on problem solving. The mystery of Faith Donahue needed solving, which is why he'd decided to bring up

her afternoon tea. Grasping the silver tray, he resembled a butler more than the master of the house. His mastery of serving,
though, was not as smooth. The china tea service rattled, cream
splattering from the pitcher, scones and treats balanced precar-
iously on a tilted plate. He barely made it to the bedside table
where he juggled the tray before setting it down.

"And what do I owe such special service?" Faith asked as she
watched him struggle. She sat up in bed, tucking the quilt in to
the high neck of her flannel gown.

He brushed a stray hair back from his brow. "Bridget was preoccupied so I thought I'd help."

She eyed the tray. "I see. There are two china cups. Either I'm
to expect a guest or you're planning on sharing the tea and good-
ies?"

"You, Madame, are very observant."

"Teachers have to be." She smiled. "Why don't you pull up a
chair and join me."

"Thank you." He retrieved the wicker chair and slunk his tall
form into it.

"Shall I pour?" he asked.

"Good idea. I'm still a bit shaky. The water in the bay can get
awfully frigid."

He reached for the teapot and poured two cups of steaming
jasmine tea, grateful that Bridget had measured and strained the
tea leaves beforehand.

"Cream or sugar?" he asked.

"Neither."

"I prefer my tea straight, too." He handed her a cup and saucer.

"Thanks." After taking the cup and saucer, she sipped the fragrant tea.

Observing her, he noted the delicate way she balanced the
china cup and the way her pinky stood out just so as she grasped
the delicate handle. For all of her idiosyncrasies, she was still feminine. He lifted his cup to his lips and sipped. After, he picked up
and passed the plate of scones and tartlets.

"I didn't realize how domestic men of your era were," she commented. "I expected them to be quite chauvinistic. Sipping tea with and serving sweets to ladies seems out of character."

He choked, handing her the plate, and took a swig of tea.

"Sorry if I've offended you," she said.

She took a bite of scone. "These could use some Devon cream."

"I don't bake or milk cows, Miss Donahue," he said, slanting his eyebrows.

She smirked, curling her lip. "I didn't think so."

"What am I to do with you?" he mumbled.

"Keep me on as Andrew's governess."

He sat up in rapt attention. "Can I trust you not to cast a magic spell on him or make him disappear?"

"As I said before, I'm a time traveler, not a witch. If you'd be kind enough to fetch me my pack, I'll show you my credentials."

Now this he had to see. Without a word, he stood, ambled over to the wardrobe, picked up her bag, and deposited it on the bed at her side. He sat in the chair in anticipation of what she might remove next.

Faith unzipped the bag and dug deep within it. She withdrew two rolled up diplomas and handed them to him.

He hesitated before accepting the parchment documents and unrolled them.

"Bowling Green State University, Bachelor of Arts in History and in Education. Notre Dame College of Ohio, Master of Education," he read, adding, "I am not aware of these schools or their curriculum."

"Unfortunately, they were not founded until 1910 and 1922 respectively."

"How do I know that these are not fabrications?"

"Doctor, I do not know what else I can do to prove to you who I am and where I come from." She reached into her pack and withdrew her eel skin wallet. She opened it and began to pull out cards, tossing them on the bed. "Here's my identification: my driver's license, credit cards, ATM cards, shopper's cards, checkbook, cash!"

He picked up the cards and read them. They were documents, the likes of which he had never seen. They looked and felt as if they had come from another world. Even the currency had unusual engravings, though the denominations and the designation, "United States of America" were convincingly real. He felt a fluttering in his chest, a lump and dryness in his throat.

Faith took his cup and filled it with tea, handing it to him. "You could use this," she offered.

He looked up at her through glazed eyes. "I could use something stronger."

His hands shook so badly that the china cup danced in the saucer as he took it from her. He could barely draw the cup up to his lips, he was trembling so much. After emptying the cup, he set it down.

"I…I don't know what to say." He rose from his seat. "You'll have to excuse me. There…there's so much for me to digest. I need to think."

"I understand," she said.

He backed away from the bed and from her. "Please, make yourself comfortable.

No more vanishing acts, please. Our discussion about your employment here is not over. Understand?"

"Yes, sir."

Bridget thought it odd that the good doctor would take a sudden interest in Miss Donahue. Ever since her miraculous return, he had treated her like a houseguest.

Allowing her to recover in the guestroom, having meals sent up, and showering her with attention gave her pause. He even served her afternoon tea. When the good doctor descended the stairs, he was not carrying the tea tray. Instead he was as pale as a ghost and rushed to his office where he slammed the door shut.

Bridget decided that it was fine time she paid a visit to Miss Donahue.

"My, oh my, you about scared the daylights out of me," Bridget said, hands on her ample hips as she waddled into Faith's room.

Faith looked up at her as if perplexed.

"Did you think I'd just leave without saying goodbye?" Faith winked.

"You were right about the earthquake and fire. The good doctor was out of his mind with confusion after your predictions came true. What's all this talk about your vanishing before his very eyes? Master Andrew kept ranting and raving about it."

"It's a long story, Bridget. All that matters is that I'm back and I'm here to stay."

Bridget stood hovering beside the bed as Faith sat zipping up the backpack and wondered about its contents. Faith seemed intent on keeping them secret from her.

"Your return has caused quite a stir. The good doctor was beside himself. From the moment he picked you up from the foyer floor, he's been keeping a vigil over you. I just think he wants to uncover the mystery behind your power."

"At least he's not interested in conducting an alien autopsy," Faith whispered under her breath.

"What ma'am?"

"Tell me, has Master Andrew been informed of my return?" She thought of the elderly man in the nursing home and blinked back tears.

"Not yet, ma'am. I'm certain that when he finds out he'll be scampering in here, jumping all over you. He's missed you so."

"I've missed him. Tell me, what has become of Miss LaDue?"

"My, oh my. She's been in quite a state. Though her family home was untouched by the earthquake, authorities decided to dynamite Nob Hill to contain the fire. The LaDue's had to evacuate. There was no time to move out their belongings. They lost everything. Poor girl joined her family on a ferry to Oakland. Imagine, the LaDue's having to rely on the charity of relatives?"

"Perhaps it will teach her some humility," Faith mumbled.

"Hardly. The girl just has one more thing to complain about. I don't know what the doctor sees in such a contrary girl."

"The engagement's still on?" Faith asked, her expression turning sullen.

"Oh yes. To lighten her spirits, the good doctor is hosting a betrothal party here the Saturday after next. A wedding date is to be announced at last."

"I see," Faith replied.

"The doctor is so honorable and intent on marrying the girl even through her misfortune. I'm sorry you had to return to such news." Bridget gazed at her, trying to read her reaction.

"The news is hardly new. Such is life," Faith said without emotion.

After spending another day in bed as a precaution, Faith was allowed to walk about the house and in the garden. Her strength returned quickly and soon she was back to chasing Andrew about. The little bundle of energy was so excited to see her he couldn't stand still. He clung to her, refusing to leave her side, fearful that she might once again vanish. She was beginning to feel like Mary Poppins, the governess with magical, mystical powers. She wasn't officially his governess. Doctor Forrester hadn't given her a final answer. As a matter of fact, she hadn't seen him since their encounter with her personal documents.

He had been avoiding her. She wasn't sure if it was out of fear or out of having to admit that he believed her.

"Miss Donahue, I want you to be my governess forever," Andrew said, grasping her hand as they strolled down Sacramento Street. His dark eyes beamed up at her with longing.

"It's your father's decision," she replied. Her future was contingent upon his decision. She crossed her fingers that destiny was on her side.

"What, pray tell, is my decision?" Doctor Forrester's dusky voice boomed behind them.

Faith stopped in her tracks, taken aback. She drew her free hand up to her chest, as if to stop the thumping of her heart. She turned to face him.

"You frightened me. Must you always be in the habit of sneaking up on people?"

He laughed, dimples forming and teeth glistening.

"Papa!" Andrew cried. He released Faith's hand and raced toward his father.

Doctor Forrester reached down and picked up his son, lifting him overhead and over his shoulders for a piggyback ride.

"I wasn't sneaking up on you," the doctor said, gazing at Faith. "After arriving home, I spotted you both and decided to surprise you."

"A surprise, indeed."

"Will Miss Donahue be my governess forever?" Andrew asked, lifting up his father's straw boater and pulling at his father's hair.

"We'll see, son." His eyes locked on to Faith's. "We'll see."

She drew a deep breath, looking away to avoid his intense gaze. "So, tell me doctor, now that the fire's out, how are the survivors coping?"

"As you well know from your study of history, Miss Donahue, the residents of San Francisco are quite resilient. There's a great deal of talk about rebuilding. Life will go on."

"Indeed it will."

"You should know," he said.

She didn't miss the bite in his tone. She held her tongue. She had been doing a great deal of that lately. Fearful of losing her position, if she still had one, and leaving the only home she knew, she was fearful of somehow sabotaging her future. She felt like a skater on thin ice, afraid of making a move for fear of sinking. What if, by chance, she was being overly cautious, altering the course of her destiny? What if Doctor Forrester did not fall in love with her and, instead, married Miss LaDue? Where would that leave her? Would she be transported back? Would she be forever lost back in time? She shuddered at the thoughts racing through her mind.

"Are you all right?" Doctor Forrester asked.

His voice rescued her from her morose thoughts. She snapped out of her funk and nodded.

"For a moment there you looked as though you were taken ill. Look at you, you're shivering."

They stopped walking.

She rubbed her arms with her hands. "Just a slight chill, nothing to be the cause of concern."

"We can return to the house if you desire." He reached up, grabbed Andrew, and lowered the boy to the ground.

"No cause for alarm. I'll be fine," she assured him.

He unbuttoned his double-breasted casual jacket and, without asking, slipped it over her shoulders. The act made her shiver more. The nubby jacket still held his warmth and masculine scent of mint and spice.

"There, that should help." He perused her, and with a satisfied smile, he took Andrew's hand and continued their stroll.

Andrew reached up with his free hand and grasped Faith's, walking between them.

Faith looked down at the child and up at his father. Together they looked like the epitome of turn-of-the-century domesticity, much like the old faded family photograph she kept hidden. All that was missing was the little girl. The thought of it made her nerves unravel and shiver all the more.

"I have a patient to check in on," the doctor said, stopping before a sprawling Eastlake style home.

"I don't see your bag," Faith said, noting the absence of the black leather satchel he carried on medical calls like an extra appendage.

"Fanny Jamison has asked to meet Andrew. She's a lonely old widow, stubborn and healthy like an ox, though she'd have you believe she's at death's door. I think she creates maladies just to coax a visit from me."

"I see that it's effective." She grinned.

"I'm a sucker for old ladies." He winked as he led them up the warped wooden steps on to a slanting porch.

"What was that for?" she asked.

"According to your own calculations, you are, after all, many decades older than me." He winked again.

Faith stared at him as he rapped on the front door. He believed her? She shook her head.

Footsteps shuffled on creaking floors inside the house. The latch clicked and the door opened just a crack.

"Doctor Forrester," the deep voice of a frail, petite dowager greeted, opening the door to get a better look at those standing on her porch. "And I see that you brought the family."

"Mrs. Jamison, we were strolling by and I thought we'd call on you." He removed his hat and held it at his side.

"You are most welcome to come and visit, especially since you brought that dear little boy I've heard so much about." Her smile was warm even with the wide gaps in her teeth. She opened the door and waved her gloved hands. "Do come in. I'm not long for this earth. I need to enjoy callers while I still can."

Dressed in head–to–toe black taffeta, a knit black shawl draped over her shoulders, and a frilled lace cap fitted on her tiny head, she looked like a figure out of a painting. Grandma Moses, perhaps, Faith thought.

Mrs. Jamison led them through the foyer, its wood floors scuffed, the burgundy flocked paper peeling away from the walls. She pointed to the parlor. Floral wall covering in hues of vermilion, lemon–chrome, celestial blue, and cream was faded and water–stained. The scattered Persian rugs were threadbare. Furnishings were scuffed and dusty. A fire blazed in the hearth adding to the stifling heat in a room that probably had never had a window opened. The scent of lemon verbena, wood smoke, and the stuffy air was suffocating.

"Won't you please sit and join me for tea?" Mrs. Jamison asked, making it sound more like an order.

Faith smoothed her skirt and sat in a low parlor chair. The springs pinched even through the thick fabric of her skirt.

Doctor Forrester sat in a nearby gentleman's chair, holding Andrew on his lap.

Before positioning herself on the rosewood sofa, Mrs. Jamison reached down to Andrew and pinched his cheek.

"What a cute one you are. A handful I can tell," she said.

Andrew rubbed his cheek with a smirk.

"I wasn't aware of you having taken a wife," Mrs. Jamison said, surveying Faith with raised eyebrows and inquisitive gray eyes.

Before the doctor might answer, Mrs. Jamison reached back and pulled on a tapestry cord. "Daisy is too deaf to answer the door but can still hear the bell."

Faith watched the woman in fascination. She half expected Lurch from the *Addams Family* to appear at any moment from the shadows.

"How old are you son?" Mrs. Jamison turned her attention to Andrew.

Andrew looked up at his father.

"He's four," the doctor replied.

"Can't the boy speak for himself? Cat got your tongue?"

Andrew stuck out his tongue. His father nudged him.

"I'll be five in July," Andrew replied.

"A big boy." She turned to Faith. "I see, Mrs. Forrester, that you have the patience for a widower and his son."

After casting a glance at the doctor, Faith answered, "I'm sorry to disappoint you, Mrs. Jamison, but I'm merely Andrew's governess."

The old woman scoffed, looking at the doctor and the child squirming on his lap.

"Doctor Forrester, does Andrew's governess accompany you on all your calls?"

Ian Forrester appeared at a loss for words. His faced paled and he squirmed in his seat.

"Only when Master Andrew is joining his father," Faith replied.

"I see." Mrs. Jamison arched her brows. "For a moment I was wondering who might be governed."

A thin black woman in a ratty maid's uniform and hair that resembled Don King's straight-up-in-the-air style plodded into the parlor. In her hands were a tarnished sterling tea service, china cups, saucers, and plates that rattled with her every move.

Faith leapt from her chair and was at the woman's side, assisting with the tray and its contents. Only when the tea service was securely set on a butler's table did she retain her seat.

Mrs. Jamison's eyes were as wide as saucers, while the maid cowered, thick lips trembling.

"Well, shall we have tea?" Mrs. Jamison began with a huff. She turned to Faith. "I'll pour."

As they strolled back down Sacramento Street en route home, Doctor Forrester chuckled. His eyes were focused upon Faith, who stood at his side gripping Andrew's hand.

"I honestly don't think Mrs. Jamison knew what to make of you."

Faith looked up at him. "Whatever do you mean?"

"Fanny Jamison thought she held the patent on being a strong woman. In you she met her match."

"Strong? Left on her own, Daisy would've dropped the tray. She's in no condition to serve yet alone clean up a mess."

"I felt as if I were seated between a battle of wills."

"Being helpful and speaking up can hardly be considered assertive," she said, and after giving it some thought added, "Perhaps, in this day and age it is. I keep forgetting that a woman's place is to be prim, proper, seen but not heard."

"In this day and age?"

"By now I thought you'd be convinced. Hasn't that *Merck*

Manual offered enough evidence?"

"The volume does offer some interesting reading, I'll admit."

"You haven't used it as a diagnostic tool yet?"

"I cannot chance treating my patients on theory. I must separate fact from conjecture."

"The book contains only fact, I can assure you. I can't transport you into the future to provide proof." She sighed.

"I have no desire to go anywhere. My home is in San Francisco with Andrew, here and now. My concern is treating my patients."

"I know, the ones who need hand–holding and smelling salts." She rolled her eyes.

He stopped walking and faced her. "If you haven't noticed, since you left and returned, my practice has shifted. After the earthquake and fire, I have devoted my practice to aiding the unfortunate. Those who suffered the most are benefiting from my skills and for the first time in my life I feel that I am making a difference in people's lives."

"Only now? I thought that's why one chose to become a doctor." She wonderedwhy it took a catastrophe for his concern to shift from the privileged to those less fortunate. Yet, he still planned on marrying a snobbish socialite.

"You don't understand. My father was an esteemed physician who built a practice treating those in his social circle. Sure, there are illnesses to contend with, babies to deliver, and the income lucrative. I reluctantly followed in his footsteps but always thought that I could do more. After his retirement and death, I assumed his practice. On the side, I would go out and treat the destitute, my only payment the personal satisfaction of making a difference in a life. After the quake and fire, I've spent hours out in the parks, doing all that I can to help and heal without giving thought to income." He put out his hands. "I am gifted. My hands heal. Is it not a doctor's role to heal the sick? Are the wealthy the only people entitled to medical treatment? I say not."

She smiled. "Doctor Forrester, I never thought I'd see the day when you were humble."

He laughed. "You don't know me well enough."

"I'm now glad just knowing you." She looked up at him, meeting his gaze. A smile glowed on her oval face.

"Did anyone ever tell you that you have a lovely smile?" he asked, surveying her.

"Someone just did."

CHAPTER 19

THE FORRESTER HOME GLISTENED LIKE a jewel amongst the ruins. A delayed spring cleaning resulted in gleaming hand–scrubbed floors, clean sponged walls, aired draperies, batted rugs, laundered doilies, sparkling oiled moldings, and lemon waxed furniture. The scent of lemons and fresh air wafted throughout the home. Lamp fixtures were polished, globes shimmering from a vinegar and water wash. Dimmed gas lamps and flickering candles warmed the wood and tapestry adding a refined elegance to the indigo dusk.

Hired wait staff in starched uniforms marched around the room like penguins, serving steaming hors d'oeuvres and champagne to mingling guests in the parlor. Men in dapper frock coats and creased striped trousers posed with women in couture creations by Worth and Drecoll, sheath gowns in muted tones and "Alice" blue, elbow–length gloves, and ostrich feathers fluttering in their hair.

After the chaos of the earthquake and fire, the prenuptial soiree for Doctor Ian Forrester and Miss Constance LaDue was one of the first social events held in the city. There was a renewed sense of hope in San Francisco and what better way to anticipate the future than with an upcoming wedding. Neighbors, friends, and the elite ousted from their Nob Hill mansions gathered at 92 Sacramento Street to reminisce about the past and celebrate the future.

Faith accompanied Andrew, introducing him to guests, as the

doctor had requested, making sure that he minded his manners and was a cordial little gentleman.

Andrew snickered at all the fussing and fawning over him. He swiped damp kisses from his cheeks and stuck out his tongue more than once behind a guest's back. Faith reprimanded him and removed a handmade slingshot and dried peas from his back breeches pocket. Faith knew that the boy hated being doted upon by strangers. To keep him in line she promised him sweets before bedtime. Bribing children, she knew, was looked down upon by Doctor Spock, but with Andrew it was the only thing that assured proper behavior. Besides, Faith surmised, Doctor Spock had yet to be born.

As she controlled Andrew, Faith could feel Doctor Forrester's eyes set upon her. She wasn't sure if it was his son's angelic behavior or something else that prompted him to take notice. Faith purposely ignored his gaze, instead concentrating on her charge. Inside, though, her stomach fluttered and warmth radiated within her. Thoughts of her destined future danced in her mind. She wondered if she should be happy or frightened by it.

The doctor's gaze did not go unnoticed by Miss Constance LaDue who clung to the man like Saran Wrap. She was ever the proper fiancée. Dressed in a virginal white silk gown with pale pink sash, her pompadour hairstyle adorned with a fragrant gardenia, she was all sweet and prim. Her kidskin–gloved hand rested on the doctor's arm as she batted her wispy lashes up at him.

The girl nauseated Faith.

As if Constance knew, she cast a superficial smile at Faith, eyes burning with the desire to have Faith dismissed as Andrew's governess and out of her life. Faith swallowed hard. What if the girl had more influence on the doctor than she surmised? After all, the wedding was still planned. What if he did dismiss her as Andrew's governess? How would destiny kick in? If destiny could be altered, where would it leave her? She placed her hands on Andrew's narrow shoulders to suppress the trembling.

"I propose a toast," a stout, gray–bearded man announced, his robust voice startling Faith from her thoughts.

A hush fell over the room as guests formed a tight circle around the man, Doctor Forrester and Miss LaDue. Waiters scurried, pouring frothing champagne into crystal goblets. Bubbles danced in the amber liquid, reflected by flickering candlelight and gas lamps, in the thin glass. A goblet was thrust at Faith. She grabbed it, tilting the glass, liquid drizzling down her fingers. She suppressed the urge to lick them.

"This is a most special evening," the man continued, raising his glass. "So much adversity and misfortune has affected our lives of late, it is with great pleasure that we gather together in celebration. The esteemed Doctor Ian Forrester and the radiant Miss Constance LaDue are formally announcing their engagement. A June first wedding is planned and I've been assured that you all will be in receipt of an invitation. Let us lift our glasses and toast this young, well–bred couple as they embark on a new life in this new city."

Doctor Forrester, with Miss LaDue attached to his arm, stepped forward. Guests raised their filled glasses. After a silent moment of sipping champagne, applause resounded. Guests gushed over the Doctor and his intended. Messages of congratulations and best wishes filled the room with joyful chatter.

Faith set down her glass of unsipped champagne. She couldn't bring the glass to her lips, couldn't even applaud. A sinking feeling cut into the pit of her stomach. Fear and doubt and the blended scent of lavender water, roses, and gardenia made her queasy. If the Doctor married the young nymphet, she would be stuck in a world where she wouldn't want to live. The walls felt as if they were closing in on her. She was hot and clammy and chilled all at once. Realizing that no one would miss them, she grabbed Andrew's arm and swooshed him out of the room.

Andrew seemed as eager to leave as she. At the news of his father's wedding, the boy broke down in tears.

"I hate her! I hate her!" Andrew cried as Faith walked him through the foyer and up the stairs. "I hate her!"

"That isn't a nice thing to say," Faith told him, though she agreed completely.

"I do hate her! She's not my mother!"

"No, she isn't. No one can ever replace your mother. She can be your friend."

He swiped his eyes with his hands. "I don't want Miss La Doo Doo as my friend. I want you as my friend."

"I'm already your friend."

"Why doesn't my papa marry you?"

She shook her head, lips parting in a partial smile. She looked down at Andrew meeting his gaze. Wisdom out of the mouths of babes.

As she tucked Andrew and his ratty bear in bed, she envied his innocence. He could go to sleep knowing he was loved and had a roof over his head. Faith knew that she would lay awake worried and confused. Her future depended upon the doctor, a man she really didn't know but was supposedly destined to marry. Ever since her first time travel adventure, she had thrown common sense out the window. Coming back seemed like the only way to escape Bradley and have an opportunity for a completely new life. Seeing Constance LaDue and the doctor had given her pause. She suddenly felt like an outsider interfering with other lives. After seeing Miss LaDue and the other ladies in their silk beaded gowns, sapphires and diamonds, she was merely the hired help. At the turn of the century, wasn't it scandalous for society gentlemen to court and wed the household help? She was just a governess now, no longer a respected teacher and wealthy urbanite.

Andrew's dark eyes were fixed on her, frightened by her somber demeanor.

"Oh," Faith said, composing herself. "I almost forgot and I bet you did, too."

"My surprise?" Andrew asked, his eyes opening wide like saucers.

Faith sat on the edge of his bed and nodded with a grin.

"Yippy!" He scooted up and sat in the bed.

Faith placed her hand in her uniform's pocket and removed chunks of crystalline rock candy. Andrew's eyes lit up.

"You can have one piece now. The rest best be saved for to-morrow."

He reached up and grabbed the chunk of clear candy and stared at it as if it were a rare diamond instead. He drew it up to his mouth and sucked on the hard, sweet morsel.

Faith watched his expression of innocent pleasure. To children, little things meant so much.

"Thank you! Thank you!" he screamed between licks. "I still don't know why you can't marry my papa."

Suddenly, his eyes focused on the doorway. He jammed the candy in his mouth, covering his face with splayed fingers.

Faith turned toward the doorway only to be met by the ebony eyes of Doctor Ian Forrester. His head was tilted, his face with a most contorted and quizzical expression. His brows were knitted, nose pinched, and eyes open wide as if he had seen a ghost.

"Sir, it was getting late so I thought Master Andrew ought to be put to bed," Faith said, heart racing. She thought for sure he would be reprimanding her on the spot for removing the boy from the party where he was a novelty.

"I quite agree," he said, softening his expression as he saun-tered into the dimly lit room.

Faith had lowered the lamp earlier to urge Andrew to sleep. Now she was grateful, for it dimmed her view of the doctor and hoped that he had a less focused view of her. As he approached the bedside, towering over her and Andrew, she was a bundle of knotted emotion. Her heart was out of control and she was giddy. It was so unlike her to have a case of the jitters. Ever since she went back through time, she was unlike herself.

"I'm sure you wish to tuck your son in for the night. I'll leave you both alone," she said, trying to appear composed. She jumped up from the bed only to find herself intimately facing the doctor. So close was she that the front of her drab gown brushed his waistcoat and she could smell his scent of spice and mint. When she looked up, her eyes caught his. For what seemed like forever they stood in intimate silence.

"Excuse me, sir," she said, stepping aside. No respectable woman of the day would ever stand so close to a man. "I…I'll leave you to your son."

"Miss Donahue, wait in the hall. I wish to have a word with you."

Faith paced the upstairs hall, hating herself. She would surely be dismissed. She not only removed the boy from his father's betrothal party, gave the boy contraband candy, she acted brazen. She was skating on thin ice and it seemed to be getting thinner and thinner at her every move.

"Miss Donahue," the doctor's dusky voice called as he closed the door to his son's room and approached her in the hall.

"Doctor?" She frowned, closed her eyes, and drew a deep breath for courage.

"Candy, huh?" he asked.

"Only one piece. I promised him. I don't break promises."

He chuckled, shoving his hands in his coat pockets. "Now I know the secret to your success and why Andrew holds you in such high regard."

"I am not in the habit of bribing children. I do believe in rewarding good behavior in difficult situations," she explained.

"I agree, the situation downstairs is most difficult." He analyzed her with his eyes. "It seems my son feels that I am planning to marry the wrong woman."

"Children, they say the silliest things," she said, trying to catch her breath, trying to make light of the topic. His eyes were x–raying her and she began to fidget in place.

"Children are more perceptive than most adults," he said. He removed a hand from his pocket and began to stroke his chin. As he pondered her, he asked, "What is your opinion?"

"About…what?"

"Am I betrothed to the wrong woman?"

She took a step back. "Doctor, it is truly your personal decision."

"I am asking you the question."

She shifted her gaze from his dark eyes to the floor. She had to shake the urge to fling herself into his arms and to kiss him. His magnetic gaze, the way he stood just a little too close, the turn in the conversation, was having a strange effect on her. She couldn't blame it on the champagne. She didn't touch it. Though destiny revealed that she was to marry him, this was the first inkling of romance she felt. It was as if his eyes were hypnotizing her into fulfilling fate. Yet, she had to look away in fear. So much had gone wrong in her life she wasn't sure what was right anymore.

He interrupted her thoughts. "Miss LaDue is young and beautiful. She is charming, of good breeding, and dutiful."

"You describe her like a pedigreed dog," Faith mumbled.

He smiled. "Ah, but dogs have spontaneity, the desire for fun and play, an independent streak."

"I'm sure she can fetch and come when called," Faith said to herself. She could envision Constance LaDue as a groomed French poodle, clipped and pouffed in white, with a diamond–studded collar.

"Apparently, she has what you seek in a wife or you wouldn't be formally engaged to her," Faith said, looking straight at him.

"She does have the qualities a successful doctor should seek in a wife."

"Doctor, I think, though, one important quality is missing here."

He tilted his head. "What is that?"

"Love."

"Love?" He choked out the word.

"I'm not very familiar with courtship in the higher classes in 1906, but in the future, love plays an integral part in every successful relationship." She kept looking at him to gauge his reaction.

He began to fidget. Catching himself, he clasped his hands behind his back and began to pace. "Love can come with time and patience."

"And one can grow old waiting," Faith replied.

"You seem to be an expert on the subject. Have you ever been in love or are you still waiting?" He stopped to face her.

"I thought I was in love once. I was really too young and naïve to understand that true love is so much deeper and meaningful, heart and soul conjoined." She thought of Brad and how she fell for his good looks, charm, and earning potential. She should have been looking into his heart for integrity, respect, and honesty.

"Wisdom from a sage."

"Why?"

"You do claim to be from one hundred years in the future."

"When, Doctor, will you believe it's not a claim but a fact?"

He winked. "We'll have to continue this conversation. The hour is late and I must bid my guests adieu."

CHAPTER 20

ANDREW AWAKENED THE MORNING AFTER the betrothal party shrieking in agony. Faith rushed into his bedroom thinking that her young charge was frightened over a nightmare. The little boy's arms flailed out as he tossed his head, writhing in his bed. His face was flush with a rash, his trembling lips blue. Tears streamed down his cheeks.

"Andrew, Andrew," Faith said in a soothing voice, sitting on the bed and reaching down to grasp his wrists. "Calm down and tell me what's wrong."

He blinked back tears, looking up at her. He contorted his face in pain.

"What's wrong?" Faith asked, growing concerned.

"My throat hurts! Make the fire stop!" he squeaked.

"You have a sore throat?"

"Yes."

She released his wrists. He immediately placed his tiny hands around his neck, as if wanting to choke himself. "It hurts! Make it stop!"

"What hurts?" a concerned voice called from the hallway. Faith peered over her shoulder to see the doctor. He stood in the doorway dressed in a double-breasted wool worsted suit, matching bowler hat in his hand. As he breezed into the room, the fresh green scent of the outdoors entered with him. Faith was grateful that he had come home at a time when his services were needed. Faith rose from her seat and moved over to the side to allow the doctor space. He sat next to his son on the bed. He placed the palm of his hand on the boy's forehead.

"He's burning with fever," the doctor said, wrinkling his forehead, knitting his brows.

"He's been complaining of a sore throat," Faith explained.

The doctor touched his son's neck, feeling the lymph nodes. "His throat is swollen."

"Sounds like a touch of the cold or flu," Faith said, "Shall I get him some hot tea with honey? Oh, and by the way, I do have a bottle of Tylenol, a pain reliever. We can probably split a tablet in half to lower the dosage."

Doctor Forrester looked up at her, a fever erupting in his eyes. "My son is ill and you have the audacity to bring up your magical quackery?"

"Say what you will, I'm just trying to help."

"You can help by telling Bridget to prepare a mustard bath and bring up some warm water to sponge the boy's face. I'll prepare a tincture of guaiac and glycerine for his quinsy."

"Quinsy?"

"Sore throat. Are you just going to stand there or are you going to make yourself useful?" He was staring at her.

"I'm going." She moved toward the door.

Instead of feeling better, Andrew grew worse. Faith thought it had to do with the archaic medical treatment. Who had ever heard of tying a slice of bacon around the neck and sprinkling it with black pepper to cure a sore throat? Doctor Forrester grew worried when his son's neck grew stiff and sore and he had difficulty swallowing. After examining the boy's throat and tonsils, he grew suspicious. He swabbed the boy's throat and analyzed the secretions under his microscope.

Faith encountered the doctor in the downstairs foyer. His face wore the pallor of death and fear glistened in his eyes. An unshaven shadow of whiskers masked his face.

He looked confused and helpless.

"I should have known," he said in anguish, hands rolled in fists at his side. "The gray membrane lesions of the throat are always a sign. I couldn't believe it. I didn't want to instill panic."

"What's wrong? What is it?" Faith asked, her heart sinking to her stomach even before she heard his explanation.

The doctor led her into the library and slid the doors closed. His lips trembled as he spoke. "Andrew is very ill and this house must, at once, be secured under quarantine. The guests at my betrothal party and any patients I have visited since must be sent notice before an epidemic occurs. I don't know how he caught it."

"What is it?"

"Diphtheria. Andrew has diphtheria."

Faith was confused. "I don't understand. I was vaccinated for it as a child. No one gets diphtheria anymore," she said. Remembering time and place, she threw her hands up to cover her mouth. She gasped. "Oh, no! Vaccinations weren't administered to prevent it in 1906!"

He stared at her, as perplexed as he always was when she mentioned her relationship to the future, the future she claimed to come from.

"Woman, don't you know that vaccinations are considered quackery, especially the antitoxin for diphtheria? They cause, not prevent disease? The diphtheria is not only deadly, it is highly contagious."

Faith didn't know what to say. The doctor began to pace the floor like a wild man, pumping his fists in the air. "Why Andrew? Why? Isn't it bad enough that I lost his mother? I can't lose him. He's a part of her, a part of me. He's all that I have."

The anguish in his voice made Faith's heart quicken. The desperate look in his eyes and the tears that soon poured forth made her swallow hard. She let him rant on about the unfairness of the situation and of a father's love for his son.

He sunk into a leather chair, spent from a grief as near to that of death as one could get. Hands in his hair, he cried, "I'm cursed. Truly cursed."

Faith couldn't stand by any longer. She went to his side and placed her hands upon his quaking shoulders, rubbing them, trying to offer some comfort. He looked up at her, pleading.

"God have mercy on my soul. If Andrew dies, so shall I die."

"Andrew will not die," Faith said as if a fact. "You're a doctor and you won't let him die."

"His life is in the hands of God."

"Let those hands guide you," Faith said in a soothing yet confident tone.

He met her gaze. "I read your medical book. Desperate men perform desperate acts."

"And?"

"I am ignorant of many of the techniques and treatments mentioned. I know to prescribe bed rest and fluids, and an icepack to sooth his swollen neck. I know that recovery is slow and overexertion can be fatal. The usual treatment is a lemon juice and water gargle and a tablespoon of citrus limonum and aqua pura every two hours. In consulting your book, I do not know what penicillin or Phenobarbital are," he said, remembering how he had scoured the book in desperation, unable to sleep since his son had taken ill. His son's life was at stake and he had to do something. Doctors were supposed to be able to cure the symptoms of disease.

"You're a good doctor but you're limited by your times," she assured him. "I have some penicillin tablets. Perhaps you can cut them to reduce the dosage." She remembered how she had foraged through her medicine cabinet, throwing plastic vials in her backpack for transport back in time, knowing that some things just hadn't been discovered yet, things that could save a life. Modern technology and advances in medical science were the things she knew she'd miss most about going back in time. The assurance of a long, happy life made her content to live without.

"You have the medicine?" He gazed at her as if she had discovered a cure for cancer.

"Yes. I also think it wise that I tend to Andrew. You did say that diphtheria is contagious. The last thing we need are you and other members of this household coming down with this. I only have so much medicine. I was vaccinated. I'm immune. Vaccinations do work. You'll have to trust me, Doctor. You give me the orders and I'll carry them out. I make no promises. We just haven't a choice."

"Are you certain?" He met her determined gaze. She was stronger than he thought, or crazier. "We cannot play games with my son's life."

"If we do nothing, your son may not have a life. With proper treatment, he will at least have some hope. It's your decision."

"My hands are tied. I haven't a choice." He hung his head as if in defeat. He couldn't sit back and do nothing. He had to do everything he could to save Andrew whether it proved successful or not.

"Yes. Now, why don't you get cleaned up, eat something, and get some rest. We're doing the best we can. As Bridget says, 'Trust in God'."

During the next ten days, Andrew's room was transformed into an in–home sequestered intensive care unit. On doctor's orders, Faith suspended a blanket over Andrew's bed, forming a tent. Underneath, she placed a croup kettle, steaming with the vapor of lime water and liquor pottassae. Andrew was able to inhale the warm, moist air. Between sucking on ice cubes, and forced liquids, he was administered alternating doses of iron chlorate of potash and whiskey. The halved penicillin tablets were given as well. Faith sat at his side, reading stories, singing, holding his hand. She explained his treatment and the reason for his isolation. He was silent and accepting. When he dozed, Faith lay back in her chair for a nap. Meals and treatments were delivered outside the door. The doctor sent notes and requested feedback that Faith posted dutifully.

The mixture of old medical treatments and the new prevented the illness from growing worse. On the tenth day when Andrew began to talk again and request food, she knew that he was feeling better. The fever had abated and his color returned to normal. Though he would remain on bed rest for several more weeks, both Faith and the doctor knew he was on the road to recovery. The room was thoroughly disinfected and aired out, the bedclothes boiled. A sense of renewal penetrated Andrew's bedroom as well as their lives.

"I don't know what to say," Doctor Forrester told Faith as they exited Andrew's room, closing the door behind. "Thanks to your care and therapies, he's improved. I still don't understand you or your magic but it has saved my son's life. I shall be forever grateful."

A lump formed in his throat as he glanced at Faith and humility filled his heart and soul. A woman, a purported time traveler, had saved his beloved son's life. There was no doubt in his mind that if she were not a member of his household, Andrew would have died. Her magic pills, the antibiotics of the future, cured the boy. The woman was changing his life in more ways than he could count. He had to admit that all of the changes were proving positive.

"Thank you." Faith smiled as she accompanied him down the hall.

Having his son survive one of the time's most insidious diseases was enough to give anyone pause. They kept the secret to Andrew's miraculous recovery to themselves.

"You were with Andrew day in and day out and yet you never caught the disease. Truly remarkable."

"As I mentioned before, I was immunized against diphtheria and others."

"Others?"

"Yes, whooping cough, smallpox, and polio. I've even had a tetanus shot. When I visited Africa years ago, I had vaccines for typhoid, yellow fever, and hepatitis."

"Interesting, though I don't understand. Studies have shown that current vaccines, antitoxins, are ineffective. Only recently, has the government passed a Food and Drug Act to establish minimum standards for the standardization and purity of vaccines and drugs, which may prove many to be effective."

"In the not–to–distant future, they will be proven effective and accepted as modern medical practice," she said.

"I will have to read my new medical guide more carefully," he said, and turning to her, "or ask you more questions."

She laughed.

He stopped walking and turned to face her. He looked down at her, eyes brimming with sincerity. "Thank you for the care you provided Andrew. You've gone well beyond the call of duty. You put your life on the line for my son. I couldn't live without him."

"I love Andrew, too."

"You do?" He placed his hands on her shoulders.

She nodded, looking up at him. "If I had borne him, I couldn't love him more. I know that's not what a governess should feel—"

"Shh...you're not the average governess."

His eyes captured hers and he wanted to melt. He was speechless. Could he actually be feeling something for her? Something beyond being a concerned and grateful employer?

He took her arm and led her down the hall to the landing of the narrow curving stairwell that led up to the servant's quarters. He gazed up at the stairs that led to her tiny attic room and looked at her.

"I imagine you're weary. You've been putting your own needs aside for Andrew," he said.

"Just doing what was best."

"For all that you've done to protect me and my household, from earthquakes and fires, to illness, I fear I'll never be able to adequately repay you. Good night, Miss Donahue." He took her hand in his, lifted it up and bent to plant a tender kiss on her fleshy palm. He released her hand, cast a brooding gaze her way, turned, and walked away.

CHAPTER 21

MISS CONSTANCE LADUE SWOOSHED INTO the house like a petite tornado. Her gaze darted about the foyer, noting the floor, the wall covering, and the furnishings. Waving her gloved hands, she announced, "I shall have my decorator come forthwith to advise."

Miss LaDue and her lady's maid arrived at 92 Sacramento Street for an extended visit. By the number of steamer trunks removed from an accompanied wagon, she appeared outfitted for an extended grand tour of Europe. Miss LaDue had been insistent upon thoroughly touring the home and planning for her future in it. Bridget, perceptive as she was, knew that the household was in trouble the moment she stepped into the foyer.

"Tsk, tsk," Miss LaDue added, peeking into the parlor. "This room is an abomination. The furnishings are as common as those ordered from Sears. There is so much work to be done. I wish to go to my room."

"Yes, ma'am," Bridget said, pointing upstairs.

Constance LaDue pivoted to face the mahogany stairwell. Her driver struggled with her trunks in the foyer, contemplating the steep stairs. Her French lady's maid sashayed up the stairs, ahead of her mistress, with a pitcher of water.

"I must get out of these wretched clothes," Constance complained. "The dust from the journey is just unbearable. I detest motorcars. They are such disagreeable and filthy objects."

Bridget choked, knowing that the "journey" wasn't that long.

With her duster, veiled hat, and gloves, dirt didn't have a chance to settle on the girl. Bridget held her tongue, rolled her eyes, and led the "guest" upstairs to the guestroom. She silently prayed that the girl would not become a permanent resident of the household. She assured herself that miracles do happen.

The coiled wire cha–changed as it made its way down the oriental runner covered treads of the front staircase. Like an alien being, it made its descent just as planned by Andrew. He sat at the top of the stairs suppressing giggles, his pudgy hands covering his mouth.

A blood–curdling scream erupted in the foyer, amplified by the high ceiling, bouncing off the walls like the Nerf ball Faith had given Andrew the day before. Miss LaDue stood shrieking as the Slinky Faith had also given the boy made its way to the bottom of the steps. Her hands trembled as she pointed to the strange wire object that seemed to have a will of its own.

Faith was the first to arrive on the scene. Seeing that the child's toy was the cause of concern, she looked up the steps to meet Andrew's animated gaze. She shook her head and bent over to pick up the Slinky. She compressed the wire toy into its closed state and held the coiled cylinder in her hand.

"You, you touched it!" Constance screamed, stepping back from Faith in fear of her.

"It's only a child's toy." Faith sighed and called up the stairs, "Andrew, come down here this instant."

In sheepish hesitation, the lad came down the stairs. When he saw Miss LaDue he began to laugh out loud.

Constance was not amused. Her pale complexion turned sunburn red. She wagged her forefinger at Andrew. "You are a wicked little boy!"

"He means no harm," Faith assured. "Andrew's just a little boy bent on fun and amusement."

"At my expense." Constance smoothed her skirt, regaining her composure and her attitude.

"Andrew, I think you owe Miss LaDue an apology," Faith said, turning to face her ward.

"I'm sorry Miss LaDue," Andrew said in a squeaky, mocking voice.

"Okay, here." Faith handed him the Slinky. "I told you not to play with it around guests. Now, take it to your room at once."

"Yes, ma'am." Andrew grabbed the toy and scurried upstairs.

"I want to warn you," Constance began when Andrew was out of sight. "Once the good doctor and I are wed, we will no longer be in need of your services."

"That will be the doctor's decision," Faith said, staring down at the childlike woman.

The girl's eyes blazed. "I shall make it his decision. You shall be paid a month's wages, a most generous offer. In return, you shall have no further contact with Andrew, the doctor, or any member of this household."

"Is the doctor in agreement of these terms?"

"He shall be. I'll make certain of it." Constance gathered her skirts, turned, and walked into the parlor without another word.

Bridget appeared from the dining room, wiping her hands in her starched apron. "My, my what made her jump out of her skin?"

"Just a child's toy."

"And a child's nanny?" Bridget's eyes locked with hers.

Doctor Forrester didn't arrive home from his medical rounds until evening. After cleaning up in his bedroom and changing into his dinner suit, he came down to the dining room. Upon his arrival, Faith was just getting Andrew settled in his seat. A pressed linen cloth in ivory covered the table set with a china dinner service and sterling set. Crystal glasses glittered in the dim gaslight.

Ivory roses with a bouquet of baby's breath in a cut crystal vase created an elegant centerpiece. Faith wanted to barf. All of it was set to impress the pampered Miss LaDue. She looked up to meet the doctor's bewildered gaze. She realized that she must have been smirking. Faith couldn't wait to leave. Bridget had assured her that she would listen discreetly to the dinner conversation. They knew that the girl would exaggerate her arrival and the Slinky incident to the good doctor.

Just as Faith was prepared to make a hasty retreat, Constance LaDue breezed into the dining room. Her ivory gown matched the tablecloth and her hair was adorned with a spray of roses and baby's breath. Faith had to hand it to the girl, she had an efficient maid who previewed the dining room and dressed her accordingly.

Ignoring Faith, Constance batted her lashes at the doctor, turning just enough to show off the cut of her gown. The doctor stood to pull out her chair. With a broad smile, Constance eased herself down into her seat.

Suddenly, Constance leapt out of her chair, shrieking. She jumped around as if fire ants attacked her. The doctor rushed to her side. Looking at her seat, he bent over to retrieve a neon blue Nerf ball.

Andrew laughed so hard his face was beet red, his eyes gushing with tears of victory.

Doctor Forrester, trying to appear concerned and attentive to Constance, suppressed a grin. He cast a glance from Andrew's amused smile to Faith's awed surprise.

"The boy must be taught proper behavior. He is run wild. He is more an animal than a child!" Constance ranted and raved, flailing her arms.

"His name is Andrew and he's my son," the doctor said, squeezing the Nerf ball.

"Doctor, that woman is evil," Constance accused, pointing a gloved finger at Faith. "She is corrupting the boy!"

Doctor Forrester turned from Constance to his son. "No toys

at the dinner table."

"Yes, Sir," Andrew replied, regaining his composure.

"Shall we have dinner?" the doctor asked.

He walked over toward Constance and pulled out her chair. She inspected it thoroughly before being seated.

As Faith moved to exit the dining room, the Doctor called, "Miss Donahue."

Faith turned just in time to catch the Nerf ball he tossed her way. She caught the ball and the doctor's eye. He winked.

Faith made a point to avoid Constance LaDue as much as possible during the girl's visit. This was a difficult task because the girl seemed to be everywhere. Constance had commissioned her mother's favorite interior decorator to assist with her plans for the Forrester home. The man, as flamboyant and pompous as a peacock, paraded around the house after his client. He was given a room–by–room tour, noting the changes Miss LaDue desired. She seemed determined to erase every memory of Doctor Forrester's late wife and everything he had held dear.

"I prefer gold flocked wall covering in the parlor. The molding must be repainted and gilded. I want the floors buffed. The chandelier must be Moorish–style. I insist that the mantel be removed and replaced," Constance informed her decorator who listened attentively and nodded in agreement with her every suggestion.

Faith was settling Andrew in for his afternoon nap when Constance and her stuffy decorator, in his cut velvet frock coat, barged into the boy's room. The doctor followed behind like a forlorn puppy.

"Master Andrew is being readied for his nap," Faith scolded, annoyed that the girl would interrupt without any consideration. "He should not be disturbed."

"Perhaps, we should return later," the doctor said.

"I am to be his mother soon. I am the one who is to deter-mine whether Andrew is being disturbed or not." Constance said, staring at Faith.

Constance scanned the painted walls of the boy's bedroom, ignoring Andrew completely. "This room would do nicely as a baby's nursery. It adjoins a room that would be suitable for a nursemaid."

The decorator nodded in agreement.

"Nursemaid?" the doctor asked, startled.

"Why, of course. You wouldn't expect me to nurse and fuss with a baby. It is my duty to give birth to a baby not to raise one. That is what hired help is for," Constance explained in an animated and determined fashion, her face a block of unyielding stone.

The doctor looked like an agitated bear prepared to pounce and growl. His hands were clasped behind his back, his face wrinkled in a scowl.

"Where would I sleep?" Andrew asked, jumping up from his bed. "This is my room!"

"Of course it is, son," the doctor assured.

"Only until the boy is sent off to boarding school," Constance added. "He is almost that age."

"Boarding school?" the doctor asked, biting his lip, to hold back words better left unsaid at the moment.

"Why, of course." Miss LaDue batted her lashes and cast a sweet curved smile in his direction. "You do prefer the boy to become a gentleman, don't you? He can't remain a sissy hiding behind his governess."

The doctor's face turned red, his eyes burning embers. Faith half expected smoke to rise from the top of his head.

"Miss LaDue, we need to talk...alone," the doctor said. He took her by the arm and moved her out of the room.

Miss LaDue's protesting voice squealed as the doctor led her down the hall and down the staircase.

The decorator cleared his throat. "I don't believe my services will be required at this moment. Perhaps, you can inform Miss LaDue that I've gone to meet with another client and shall keep in correspondence."

"Of course," Faith said. If it were up to her, his services would never be required.

"Good day," the decorator bid as he walked from the room.

"Miss LaDue certainly overstepped her bounds this time," Faith commented.

"I hate her!" Andrew said. "I wish she'd go away!"

"You know, Andrew, that wish might just come true." Faith smiled, wondering what the doctor was telling the girl.

CHAPTER 22

FAITH AWAKENED TO THE SOUND of slamming doors, footsteps, the clatter of dragged luggage, and fussing voices. The noise cleared her head and the purring motor of a car outside her window prompted her out of bed. Without bothering to grab her robe, she scurried to her window, drawing back the curtains to observe the scene below.

Constance LaDue stood on the front walk surrounded by her steamer trunks. Attired in a duster, gloves, and veiled hat she was barking orders to the hired driver. Her maid stood nearby waving her arms in a frenzy, mumbling in French. The driver leaned against the shiny motorcar mopping his brow, ignoring the women and their tantrums. His vehicle seemed inadequate to accommodate the women and the trunks. Bridget was nowhere in sight and the doctor was conspicuously absent.

Faith smiled. Her destiny might be realized after all.

She took extra care in her toilet, fixing her hair in a flattering pompadour. The tortoiseshell comb added color to her light brown hair. Going back to natural brunette after half a lifetime as a bottle blond had taken getting used to, but maintenance was so simple. Not having to apply cosmetics was another timesaver. She was just grateful for having a decent complexion.

She dressed in the new outfit she had ordered from the Sears catalog. The embroidered white lawn shirtwaist and flounced black broadcloth and silk skirt accented her small waistline and feminine curves. After adding her jewelry, she checked herself in the washstand mirror. The effect was understated elegance. Everything in 1906 was so formal compared to the casual dressed–down new millennium. Faith felt like a little girl playing dress–up.

Andrew was already awake when she entered his room. After washing his face and hands, she helped him into his two–piece worsted suit. The brown breeches and coat matched his dark eyes. For the first time, he didn't complain about having to get dressed. He was exceptionally quiet and kept grinning from ear to ear.

"Now, tell me what's going on?" Faith asked. "This is so unlike you."

"I chased her away," Andrew said, waving his hand in victory.

"Who?" Faith didn't have to ask but did anyway.

"Miss La Doo Doo. I hate her."

"Andrew, as I said before, that isn't a nice thing to say."

"I'm glad she's gone and I hope it's for good.

Faith grinned. She couldn't have said it better.

She escorted her charge downstairs for breakfast. As she descended the stairs and reached the foyer, she could see the doctor seated at the dining room table alone with a cup of tea. For a moment she just looked at him. Even when seated, his height and posture gave him an air of authority. His broad shoulders were clothed in the navy blue and green broken–checked pattern of his suit. A bow tie was knotted at his neck. His wavy hair was slicked back. His dark eyes looked ahead in some distant deep thought. She closed her eyes, thinking that this was how mornings were destined to be. She would be greeting her husband at breakfast. What would he be thinking? Would his thoughts be on the previous night? Would he be content with her? Would she be content with him? Were they going to fall in love and stay in love?

She opened her eyes to have Andrew gazing up at her.

"Go join your father, Andrew," she whispered, nudging the boy with her hand.

"Is that Miss Donahue?" the doctor called, turning to face the foyer.

"Yes it is, Papa," Andrew replied, scampering into the dining room and into his father's outstretched arms.

The doctor pulled the boy on to his lap and wrapped his arms around him.

"Miss Donahue, please come in," the doctor invited.

Faith sashayed into the dining room. The table was set simply with a linen tablecloth and everyday china. The setting was for three.

"Sir?" Faith asked, nerves fluttering, knowing that Doctor Ian Forrester was destined to be her new husband.

"Won't you join us for breakfast?" the doctor asked. After planting a kiss atop Andrew's head, he set his son on the floor.

Andrew scurried to his chair and Faith helped him up into his seat.

"Are you sure?" Faith asked.

"Will you please sit?" the doctor ordered, pointing to a chair next to his, across from Andrew.

"I always dine in the kitchen with the other hired help." She knew that the doctor liked to tend to his son alone during meals, a sort of bonding ritual between father and son.

The doctor set down his tea and rose. He stepped over and pulled out the cane seat chair for her. "Sit."

Faith eased herself into the chair. She unfolded her napkin and fanned it on her lap.

After pushing her chair in, the doctor took his seat. Bridget waddled into the room with a basket of steaming biscuits, setting them down on the table. She caught Faith's eye and winked, as if she could read Faith's mind. Andrew sat still and silent, a broad smile beaming from his face. When he was well behaved he appeared rather angelic.

"What are you so pleased about this morning?" the doctor asked the boy, looking at him.

"Miss La Doo Doo is gone."

The doctor sighed. "Thank heaven for small miracles."

"Will she be coming back?"

"No, Andrew, Miss LaDue will not be returning."

Andrew cheered, jumping up and down in his seat.

"Andrew, that isn't nice," Faith reprimanded, and turning to the doctor with forced sympathy, "I'm sorry to hear the news, especially after the beautiful betrothal celebration."

"It is fortunate that we discovered our differences before the ceremony."

Andrew reached for a biscuit only to drop it on the table after it burned his fingers. Faith retrieved the biscuit and placed it on the boy's plate under the watchful eye of the doctor. Bridget returned with jars of apricot jam and currant jelly, syrup, soft–boiled eggs in crystal eggcups, and platters of hotcakes and country sausage. On most mornings the doctor only requested tea and Andrew's hot porridge. Such hearty meals were reserved for guests. Though Miss LaDue was gone, the doctor insisted on a full breakfast. Having Faith seated in the dining room raised Bridget's eyebrows and a crooked grin creased her face as she served.

Faith tended to Andrew as the doctor watched intently, though pretending to eat his breakfast. She buttered Andrew's biscuit and slathered it with jam. She removed the shell from his egg, sliced his ham into edible cubes, and poured maple syrup over his hotcakes. Andrew sat patient and still. After taking care of Andrews's needs, Faith focused on her own plate. She delicately held her fork, she slowly chewed, and she sat erect and poised, knowing that he was observing her. As Faith looked up, she caught the doctor's gaze.

Looking into her eyes was like looking into the future, deep and mysterious. The future! She claimed to be from the future! He was flush and shaky and had to look   away. A woman never had such an effect on him. Even his wife, whom he loved deeply, hadn't touched him so completely. When near, Faith caused an earthquake to rattle his body as well as mind. The ensuing fire in his heart, soul, and groin was as difficult to extinguish. When

Constance was in his life, he had an excuse to avoid Faith and to deny the feelings she stirred within him. Constance was gone.

Constance was the type of woman a man in his social circle and profession was supposed to be attracted to. She was young, beautiful, wealthy, spoiled, his social equal.

Next to Faith, though, she was a mere child. Faith had the maturity, intellect, strength, caring, and spontaneity that he found stimulating and exciting. There was enough mystery surrounding her to keep him amused for decades. He chuckled at the thought. She was his child's governess, though. A relationship with her would be social and professional suicide. His smile faded into the thin line of a grimace.

After the breakfast dishes were cleared, Andrew asked to be excused. Faith rose from her seat to tend to him.

"Please stay, Miss Donahue," the doctor invited.

"I must see to Andrew's lessons."

"Let the boy frolic for a while. I would like to talk to you."

Faith hesitated for a moment and then sat.

"Bridget," the doctor called.

"Sir?" Bridget peeked out of the pantry.

"Would you please mind Andrew? I wish to speak with Miss Donahue."

"Yes, sir." Bridget retreated. Soon, her booming brogue could be heard scolding the boy.

The doctor leaned back in his chair, analyzing Faith. She sat straight in her seat, her face in profile as she glanced toward the pantry after Bridget and Andrew. Her features were delicate and classical as if chiseled by a sculptor, her complexion as ivory and smooth as fine marble. Her hair was medium brown without a hint of gray, her eyes a youthful glistening aquamarine. He tried to guess her age but was stumped. He knew she was older than Constance but younger than he, perhaps in her early thirties?

Unless, of course she was from 100 years hence, which would put her somewhere around 135 or so. He shrugged his shoulders and shook his head. Even though evidence pointed toward the theory of Faith being a time traveler from the future, he still had a difficult time accepting it as fact.

"Tell me about your world," Doctor Forrester said, his curiosity growing.

As Faith turned to face him, she straightened up in her seat, adjusting her skirt, like a witness preparing to be interrogated at the bench.

"Are you sure you want to hear about my world?"

He leaned back in his chair, crossing his arms over his chest. "I want to hear everything."

"Haven't I offered enough proof of my journey already?"

"Your picture book, the medical text, your miracle medicines, your clothing and ways, your predictions are certainly not of this place and time."

She sighed and smiled.

"At first I thought it preposterous yet I can offer no explanation. I need to learn more."

"So, you've finally come to the realization that I'm not crazy?"

He leaned forward, folding his arms on the table. "Perhaps it is I who am crazy for believing you. What you know and what you've done defy all human logic and scientific explanation."

She grinned.

"Tell me, what is society and the human condition like in 2006?"

After drawing a deep breath she began a thorough explanation of technology yet invented, of appliances yet manufactured, of shifting morals and freely casual fashion, of modern convenience and ease and economy of travel, of medical milestones, and of history yet to be made.

Beginning at the breakfast table, continuing with a long afternoon stroll and sit in the park, the discussion carried over to the dinner hour. They found themselves seated at the dining table with Bridget serving fried chicken and country ham.

The aroma of fruit and spice awakened pangs of hunger in Faith. The all–day conversation had kept her so preoccupied she had given little thought to food. She closed her eyes and savored the scent of hot comfort food. When she opened them, they were met by the doctor's dark, deep gaze. A different hunger gnawed at her and she shifted uneasily in her seat. She looked down at her plate to avoid his eyes.

"Is something wrong Miss Donahue?" he asked.

"No," she lied. Something was wrong even when destiny was proving it right. After the fiasco with Brad, she tried to keep all sexual and romantic notions buried. Time spent with Doctor Forrester, the sound of his dusky voice, his spicy mint scent, his seductive smile, and intense gaze was stirring them up.

"Miss Donahue, I have another question."

"It seems I've answered quite a few already today."

"Why did you come back in time? What explanation do you have for appearing in San Francisco in 1906 and coming into my life? Surely, you could have traveled to other times and places and touched other lives?"

Her heart stopped and she couldn't breath. She couldn't look at him and sat frozen. She was unraveling. *I came to meet you, to love you, to marry you and bear a child I so desperately want!*

"What is your theory, Miss Donahue?" He was staring through her.

"I…I don't have a theory. I don't know," she lied.

He leaned forward. "I have a theory."

"You…you do?" Her heart now was beating faster than ever and she was growing flush and faint.

"You came back to save my life," he said in a calm, unaffected tone.

"Your life?" She was staring at him with eyes wide open and mouth agape.

"Yes, several times."

"I don't understand."

"I don't expect you to. Unknown to you, before and after your arrival here, I have spent the early dawns in the shanty town South of Market tending to the poor and unfortunate. I felt it was my call to help those without as well as those with an overabundance. If not for your warning, I would have been there during the earthquake and been trapped in the midst of the fire. With the high death toll, Andrew would have surely been without a father."

"I never knew," she mumbled at the shock of the revelation.

"The second time you saved my life was when you saved Andrew's life from that wretched bout of diphtheria. If Andrew died, I, too, would be dead. I couldn't and wouldn't live without him."

She choked back tears.

"The third time was how you made me come to my senses about Constance LaDue. Comparing your attributes to hers made me realize what a mistake I was making by becoming betrothed to her. Though I was born into it, I am not a man who lives by high society's standards. Healthcare isn't something that should be bought and neither should love and happiness."

She dabbed at tears settling in the corner of her eyes.

"See, you've saved me from certain death, from smothering myself in a profession of hand–holding society matrons when my passion is in healing the less fortunate, and, in realizing that, I was about to marry the wrong person."

"I don't know what to say, Doctor Forrester." She really didn't. "I won't take credit for acts of fate."

"Then, for acts of Faith?" He reached across the table and grabbed her hand.

Her hand seemed so small and insignificant in his large, firm grasp. As he squeezed her hand, currents of electricity tingled up her arm and down her spine. She could feel the hairs rise on her neck and shivered at the effect. He was holding her hand and staring at her with equal intensity. Sparks ignited within her and seemed to arc between them. She never had been so moved in her life. No man ever made her tingle. Until now.

"Papa!" Andrew called, wriggling out of Bridget's grasp and

bolting into the dining room. "Miss Donahue!"

"Andrew!" Faith and Doctor Forrester said in unison, ex-changing a silent glance.

The doctor released her hand in time to gather his son up on to his lap and into his arms.

"I'm sorry, sir. The wee one was determined," Bridget apolo-gized. She snickered at the doctor and winked at Faith.

"No need to worry. He just takes after his father," Doctor Forrester said.

"Are you and Miss Donahue getting married?" Andrew asked.

"Why?"

"You were holding hands!"

CHAPTER 23

"SO TELL ME, IS THE governess about to get betrothed to the good doctor?" Bridget asked, hands on her hips as she confronted Faith in her attic bedroom.

Faith looked up from her seat on the lumpy mattress and stopped brushing her tangle of hair. Attired in her flannel nightgown, she was ready for bed, not interrogation.

"Well?" Bridget persisted.

"Why would you say such a thing?"

"I'm not blind."

Faith sighed. "I know it would be very hard for you to understand."

"There's a great deal I don't understand about you, Miss Donahue. One thing, though, I am certain of."

"And what's that?"

"The good doctor has taken a liking to you." Bridget raised her eyebrows, her lacy linen nightcap bobbing up and down. " I see the way he's been looking at you of late. He's been seeing more than his child's governess. I think he's seeing his child's new mother."

"Didn't he see Constance as mother material also. Where is she now?"

Bridget chuckled. "Miss LaDue is probably setting her hooks in some other unsuspecting fellow. As for you, I've always thought that you and the good doctor were meant for each other. I always felt that there was a reason for your coming into our lives."

Faith smiled. Even Bridget understood Faith's destiny. During most of her years, Faith had thought that you created your own life and future. She never understood the mysterious outside forces that propelled, like a current, sweeping one along on a charted course through life. Everything had a reason. Life wasn't just happenstance and circumstance. There was some divine plan. Somehow, she was meant to live in 1906 with Doctor Forrester, Andrew, and Bridget.

"Oh, Bridget, there is a reason for my being here with all of you," she said. " I'm starting over in a place and time where I finally belong."

Where I belong. Faith had never admitted it before but she knew it was true. Her entire life had been spent trying to fit into society. She had thought that Bradley was her key. He had turned the shy, ugly duckling farm girl entering her freshman year into a lovely, sophisticated swan by graduation. He made her feel wanted by marrying her and whisking her away to San Francisco. Teaching had opened up the diverse world to her, and Clarice had taught her about friendship and empathy.

Deep inside, though, she was the same insecure Faith who put on the public façade of confidence and social savvy. Moving away and losing her parents, and losing her marriage, made her travel full circle.

Here she was, starting over. She was back to the simple things like mousy brown hair and no make–up, back to flannel nightgowns, and drab clothes, back to dreaming about marriage and children. There was a big difference. She was older and wiser. She also knew her future and she liked what she foresaw.

After settling Andrew down for his afternoon nap, Faith wandered into the library where she liked to spend quiet time amongst the worn leather volumes amply lining the shelves. Doctor Forrester's collection was eclectic and ranged from classics like

Homer's *Odyssey* to Jack London's *Call of the Wild*. As she perused the shelves, she admired the doctor's taste in literature but what she wouldn't give for a Danielle Steele tearjerker or a James Michener historical epic.

She turned to face the doctor's mahogany desk. His wire–rim glasses lay atop an open book. Out of curiosity she moved the delicate frames, and turned over the book to see its cover. The title made her gasp, *The Time Machine* by H.G. Wells. Lying next to it was her picture book of San Francisco.

"So this is where you spend your free time?" came a voice from behind.

Startled, Faith jumped, only to meet the gaze of Doctor Forrester who stood in the doorway holding his medical satchel. His face was drawn with a four o'clock shadow shading it. His shirt collar was loose and his tie undone. He wasn't his impeccable self and she wondered why.

"Doctor Forrester, I wasn't expecting you," she said, putting down the book.

He set down his satchel and stepped into the library.

"So what are you reading today, Miss Donahue?"

"I haven't decided yet."

"You were holding a book." He approached her.

"Oh that."

The doctor walked up to the desk and glanced over at the open volume and his eyes met Faith's. "I see that you're more interested in my selection."

"Just curious, nothing more," she said, looking at him. There were dark shadows under his eyes and his lips were trembling. He looked like hell. "Doctor, is everything okay?" she asked. "You don't look well."

"I'm not well," he muttered, plopping into the overstuffed chair. He lifted his hands to his head, grasping at his hair in torment. "Oh, God!" he cried, closing his eyes as tears streamed down his cheeks.

"Can I get you some water? Some brandy?" Faith asked. She

had never seen him in such a state. He was usually so together.

"Just sit," he said, pointing to the floor at his side.

She knelt down, looking up at him. "Is there anything I can do?"

"No. No. There's nothing anyone can do. Nothing."

"At least tell me what's wrong," she prompted. "It's always better to talk things out."

He opened his blurry eyes, wiping away tears with his hands. "Oh, Faith, I'm so sorry you had to see me like this. The last time this happened was when…when." He choked on his words. "When Andrew was born. I…I couldn't save his mother and this morning I couldn't save Angelina either. It was like reliving the whole wretched nightmare."

His eyes were glazed over as he stared into space.

Faith closed her eyes and drew a deep breath for courage. The anguish of the past was coming back to haunt the present.

He continued, "She was the same age, had the same dark hair and eyes, had a difficult labor, and had delivered a healthy baby boy. She had everything to live for. Everything. She was begging me to help her but I couldn't do anything to stop the hemorrhaging. She stared at me, her eyes wide with foreboding, knowing she was dying and that I couldn't save her. I tried but I couldn't save her."

"You're only human," Faith whispered, knowing that her words were little consolation when a life was lost.

"What kind of doctor am I to sit back and helplessly watch beautiful young mothers die? What made me think I could save her when I couldn't even save my own wife? I couldn't even save Andrew's mother." He bent forward, clasping his head in his hands. His shoulders quaked as he was overcome with grief and tears.

Faith knelt and wrapped her arms around him, holding him like a mother comforting a child. "You did your best. You're not God. Only God determines who lives and who dies, when and where."

"Oh, God. Why?" he cried, reliving the memories of years ago after Andrew's mother died. He reached out and clung to Faith. He held on to her for strength as she hugged him to offer comfort.

She didn't know how long they were intertwined but she was grateful that Bridget was away to the market. Quiet was needed at times like these.

The doctor looked up, still holding on to Faith as she, in turn, held him. He sniffled, swallowing hard. "I'm sorry for putting you through all this, Faith," he said. "Thank you for being so under-standing. You probably now think of me as some sort of madman."

She looked into his glassy bloodshot eyes. "We're all allowed to be crazy once in a while. You have a reason for being upset."

He blinked. "It was like reliving the worst nightmare in my life. There's nothing as devastating as losing someone you love."

Or losing someone you think you love. Faith thought of Brad and the divorce.

His magnetic touch aroused her from her thoughts. She shivered as she met his intense gaze. Was it his touch, his eyes, or the emotions of the moment that made her tremble so?

"Thank you for being here, Faith," he murmured, drawing her into an intimate embrace.

Her arms encircled his neck as he drew her up against him. His scent of spice and mint was intoxicating. His head pressed against hers, his face buried in the nape of her neck, his breath moist and hot on her delicate flesh.

"I've never been moved to tears before at the death of a pa-tient," he whispered.

"You're only human," she said, running her fingers through his damp hair, an action that was involuntary.

"It made me realize how fragile life and love is." His hands began to pull at her hair, mussing her pompadour and chignon.

As her hair fell free to her shoulders, Faith thought she'd faint from his tender touch, the heat radiating from his body and breath, the emotion in his words and dusky voice. He was awakening the woman in her, tingling areas that had been dormant for so long she was frightened.

"Don't tremble," he whispered. "There's no reason to tremble." He raised his head to look into her glowing eyes.

For a moment their eyes melded. Two sets became one in an instant. She closed her eyes just as his lips reached down to capture hers. His mouth was lush, hot, demanding. Fleshy lips that nibbled against hers, tasting and teasing from bottom to top and back again. Just when she was getting used to his hot rhythm, he changed the pace, prying with his tongue. She willingly opened her mouth to welcome his curling tongue and salty taste. As their tongues danced and joined she was on fire.

He lowered her to the floor without stopping his mouth's seduction. Her back pressed against the Oriental rug as he rolled over her, clasping her wrists back above her head. Beneath his lithe form she was a willing prisoner.

Suddenly, rumbling footsteps and banshee screaming disrupted the tryst. Doctor Forrester jumped up and off of her, yelping in pain as tiny fists pummeled him about the head and neck. As he rose to his feet, Andrew clung to his neck kicking and screaming.

"Stop it! Stop hurting Miss Donahue! Leave her alone! Leave her alone!" Andrew was in near hysteria, his face flushed red with anger and upset.

Doctor Forrester reached up and behind trying to get his son off his back down to his feet. The child clung like an attack cat. Faith rose to her knees and up on her feet. With her heart still pulsing from hypnotic kisses, she drew a deep breath for composure. She stepped toward the doctor and reached out to pull Andrew who was practically strangling his father.

"Andrew! Andrew, let go!" she ordered, grasping the boy about the waist.

With his hands free, the boy pulled at his father's hair screaming, "I hate you! You're mean! You were hurting Miss Donahue!"

"Let go," Faith yanked at Andrew's waist until he finally released his grip on his father's neck. She lowered the boy to the floor but held him by his suspenders like a tethered dog.

Doctor Forrester rubbed his neck, shaking his head to get the kinks out. He looked down at the keg of dynamite that was his son.

"What's wrong with you, boy?" he asked.

"I won't let you hurt Miss Donahue!" Andrew stomped his feet. "I won't!"

Faith held tight to the boy's suspenders that pulled back and forth like rubber bands. Andrew's hands were curled into fists, ready to beat up his father.

"He wasn't hurting me," Faith said in a calm voice.

"Papa had you pinned to the floor! He hurt you!"

"Andrew, we were playing," Faith said, smiling. If the boy weren't so serious she would have burst out in uncontrollable laughter. The scene was one for the movies.

"Yes, we were only playing," the doctor added, rubbing his neck, wincing in pain.

"Playing?" Andrew asked, calming down.

"Wrestling," Faith said.

"You don't play with me like that." Andrew pouted.

"When you get older," the doctor said and snickered, his eyes meeting Faith's.

"I bet Bridget's back from the market and has lunch about ready," Faith said, diplomatically changing the subject. She released his suspenders and smoothed her skirt.

"Why don't you go see what Bridget's cooking?" the doctor hinted to his son.

Andrew looked up at his father with a sneer. He held his head high and marched out of the library without a backward glance.

"He thinks he's Napoleon," Faith said with a chuckle.

"He packs quite a punch." Doctor Forrester was still twisting his neck. "I must have pulled a muscle."

Faith walked up to him and placed her hand on his neck. Red welts were swelling where Andrew had tightened his grasp. The doctor had to be in pain. "May I help?"

The doctor reached back and removed her hand. "Miss Dona-hue, please keep your hands to yourself." His gaze was unwaver-ing, his eyes aglow. "You know what happened the last time you touched me."

He was so deadpan serious she began to laugh. She shook her head.

"I don't see the humor," the doctor said.

"That's because you're the one who was beaten up by a four–year–old."

"And over a woman, yet." The doctor winked.

"I'd better fix my hair and tend to Andrew," Faith said, turning toward the doorway.

"Faith?" the doctor called.

She pivoted to face him.

"We need to talk," he said in a serious tone, raking his hands through his tousled hair. They definitely had to talk.

Doctor Forrester didn't join them for lunch. Faith sat alone with Andrew in the dining room as the boy slurped his soup and munched on cold chicken. No offense to Bridget's culinary skill, but she would have given anything for a cheeseburger and fries. A chocolate milkshake would have tasted good, too.

Watching Andrew, it was hard to believe that this angelic little boy could fight and hit so hard. She surmised that the doctor was still hurting and wasn't quite ready to face his son. Bridget had mentioned that the doctor had taken to his bed for a nap. After all, he had been up all night and morning tending to the difficult delivery. She thought about the doctor and his recollection of the death of Andrew's mother and of his tattered emotional state.

She closed her eyes remembering the crush of his lips and the length of his body over hers. Just thinking about his taste and touch made her cross her legs. She couldn't help but wonder if he cared for her or was merely using her as a way to release all the pent–up tension. He did say that they had to talk. *What did he have to say?* That he was sorry and didn't mean it? That it would never happen again? She opened her eyes, confused.

Just as Bridget entered to refill Andrew's glass of milk, Andrew asked Faith, "What game were you and papa playing on the floor?"

Bridget's eyebrows shot up and she cast a glance at Faith that could have boiled the jug of milk.

Faith cleared her throat. "An adult game."

"Wrestling?"

"Yes, Andrew."

Bridget approached Faith and leaned toward her, asking with a bite in her voice, "Would you like some milk, Miss Donahue, or, perhaps something more potent?"

"The doctor may be in need of your brandy, Bridget," Faith said.

"I hit papa." Andrew was beaming as if it were something to be proud of.

"Is that so? And that's a good thing?" Bridget tilted her head, rising.

"I saved Miss Donahue."

"Saved her?"

"From papa."

"I see," Bridget smiled and mumbled, "Most women prefer not to be saved from the good doctor."

"It's a long story, Bridget," Faith said, wanting to end the conversation once and for all.

"And I will be hearing it one of these days, eh?" she asked, nudging Faith before she returned to the pantry.

The next day, Doctor Forrester left early to tend to his patients, neglected to come home for lunch, and arrived late for supper. He breezed into the dining room just in time for dessert. Bridget was scooping out strawberry trifle with dollops of whipped cream.

"Papa," Andrew greeted, lowering his head sheepishly.

Faith's lecture on never punching your father must have hit home.

"Doctor," Faith said with a forced smile. She wasn't sure how to react to him after all the conflicting emotion he seemed to evoke lately.

"My, everyone is in such a gay mood," the doctor said with a hint of sarcasm in his voice as he pulled out a chair and sat across from Faith. He fanned his napkin on his lap as Bridget plopped an abundant serving of trifle in front of him.

"No offense, Bridget, but is anything left over from the evening meal?"

"I can fry up a cheeseburger or two for you," Bridget replied.

"A what?"

"Miss Donahue helped with supper this evening. We made cheeseburgers and French fries."

He stared at the women, perplexed. "I don't recall ever having such a meal."

"It's good, papa," Andrew added, licking his lips for emphasis.

"Miss Donahue can cook, too?" he asked, glancing over to Faith and to Bridget, "I'll try this new supper."

"Yes, Sir." Bridget went through the pantry toward the kitchen.

"Is there anything you cannot do, Miss Donahue?" he asked, lifting a palm. "Don't answer. I shall fear your answer." He lifted up his forefinger as a signal to silence her.

Faith took a spoonful of trifle. Whipped cream clung to her mouth. As she licked it off her top lip, the doctor gave her the most quizzical stare. She thought he'd drool at any moment.

"I apologize for being late," he said. "I had a baby to deliver, a precious little girl. Mother and baby are doing fine." He smiled, bottom lip trembling.

"That's wonderful," Faith said, glad to hear of a happy outcome.

Maybe that's why he was nervous and fidgeting. She couldn't understand how a man who always had his act together, was cool to the point of arrogance, could be so messed up lately. He went from being Lawrence Olivier to Hugh Grant.

Bridget served his meal of a cheeseburger covered with lettuce and tomato on a homemade roll with steaming French fries. He stared at the plate and looked up at Faith. "Interesting. Is this a common meal in your world, Miss Donahue?" he asked.

"Very much so. Restaurants are devoted to it." Oh, how she missed the Golden Arches.

She watched him raise the burger up to his lips and take a juicy bite. She tingled, remembering how those same lips nibbled hers. Oh, to be that cheeseburger. She wanted to pinch herself for such lurid thoughts.

After the doctor's supper and dessert, Faith was about to excuse herself to go up to her room. The day had been long and vexing. She wanted nothing more than to go to bed to sort out the day and her thoughts.

As she rose from her chair, the doctor asked, "Faith, shall you join me for a walk in the garden? I wish to speak with you."

"The hour is getting late," she said, wanting to beg off yet curious about his intentions.

"Ah, but the night is young," he said in a low voice directed at her.

"Andrew must be tucked in for the night."

"Bridget," the doctor called. The maid appeared. "Please see to it that Master Andrew is put to bed. I have important matters to discuss with Miss Donahue."

"Yes, Sir." Bridget snickered and winked at Faith.

The doctor took Faith's arm and escorted her out to the moonlit garden. They strolled down the brick garden path shaded by oak and cherry trees and under an arbor dripping with fragrant bougainvillea. The full moon glowed above like a gazing ball and moonflowers glittered as they climbed a nearby trellis. The doctor pointed to a cast iron settee and Faith sat.

She was as nervous as a schoolgirl on a first date. Just because she was transported back in time, did she have to feel as flush and silly as a woman native to the era? The doctor pulled a matching cast iron chair next to her and settled into the narrow seat.

"Faith," he began, fidgeting with his hands. "We need to talk."

"So you've said." She clasped her hands together on her lap to hide her own nervousness.

"About the other day in the library," he began. "It wasn't my intention to be so forward. I know it wasn't proper behavior befitting a gentleman. I allowed emotion to overrule my common sense." He gazed at her, eyes hooded in sincerity and apology.

She didn't need an apology. She needed to be hugged and kissed again. She needed to touch him, to smell him, to taste him.

"Andrew doesn't know it but I deserved his wrath." He wrung his hands. "It wasn't my desire to cause you harm and I assure you, it shall not happen again."

Her face went blank. She was all geared up for a profession of love and desire, not a cool apology for an act as old as the ages.

"If we are to court, Miss Donahue, my intention is to be a gentleman."

She half expected him to rise and bow. *A gentleman?* She wanted a hot–blooded male.

She stared at him, irritation evident in her glaring eyes and pursed lips. "Doctor Forrester, you must understand that I'm not a woman of 1906 but a woman of 2006. The rules of courtship and dating are very different. What you would consider improper is acceptable in the world where I come from," she tried to explain without being blunt.

He swallowed hard. "Our differences are vast, are they not? Even in courtship?"

"Things aren't that different. Emotion, feelings are the same and I'm sure expressing them is the same just on a different level. What we did in the library is not an immoral act."

His brows shot up. "Does that mean that in your world men and women are free to take liberties with anyone they please, anywhere, and anytime without apology?" he asked.

"Yes."

He stood, ringing his hands. "I imagine that you have allowed yourself to be mauled and kissed by many a man, have you not?"

"No. I haven't. The only man who touched me was my husband and we're divorced," she admitted.

"You *are* divorced? That explains the wedding ring. I should have known, Missus Donahue." He began to pace like a trapped lion.

"Doctor, you were married. Your wife died. My ex–husband is good as dead in my eyes. He lives in the future, for Christ's sake. If you must know, he dumped me for a younger woman who had his babies." She stood to confront him. How dare he be so upset about her past marital status? "Neither of us is married now. The past shouldn't matter."

"It does concern me."

"Then Doctor, may I suggest that you find another virginal bimbo like Miss LaDue to court in the prim and proper manner to which you are accustomed." She grabbed her skirt, turned, and stomped toward the house.

He trailed after her. "I don't love Miss LaDue. I love you!"

Faith froze in her tracks. *Did he say that he loved her?*

He reached out to grasp her. He swung her around to face him. "I love you," he repeated, looking deeply into her eyes.

"Me?"

"Yes. Ever since you entered my life I've been drawn to you like a bee to a flower. You're not like the prim and proper ladies I am accustomed to. You are a lively free spirit with your own ideas and ways. You are an independent thinker and a challenge to be around. You stimulate the mind as well as the body. In the library, it hit me like a ton of bricks. I love you. I love everything about you, even the flesh–toned hose, that ugly thing you call a backpack, even those greasy cheeseburgers. I don't care if you came from the future or the moon. I still love you." In telling her, he felt a sense of relief he hadn't had all day.

"I might just faint."

"Don't become prim and proper, Faith." He wrapped his hands around her waist and drew her near until she was crushed against his chest and forced to look up into his intense eyes.

She reached up to encircle his neck with her arms. This couldn't be happening. She gazed into his eyes that glittered like the stars overhead. She was fulfilling her destiny.

CHAPTER 24

"*DO YOU LOVE HIM?*" *CLARICE asked, ebony eyes piercing.*
    "*What a silly question,*" *Faith answered, flinging her hair over her shoulder with a nonchalant flick of her wrist.*
    "*The answer is the most important in your life. Do you love him? Do you really love him? Not, do you love the fact that he's helping you escape from memories of Brad? Not, do you love him because he can father your dream child? Do you love him for the man he is and the man he will become? Do you love Doctor Ian Forrester?*"
    "Yes! Yes!" Faith answered, startling herself awake from a deep slumber and an all–too–vivid dream. "Clarice, I do love him. I really love him."
    Her words hung in the cold, midnight air. She was surprised at her admission and proclamation of love. How readily the words flowed from her lips. Touching a forefinger to her lips, she closed her eyes and lie back into the down filled pillow. There had been so few people she loved in her life. She loved her mother and father for the integral roles they played in creating and molding her. She loved Clarice for always being there through good and bad. Brad was the first man she had ever loved, her first romantic love encounter. The love of parents never dies. True friendship never ceases. But romantic love can wither, if not tended. The love she had for Brad died like a rose bush in a drought. When he stopped loving her he killed it.
    Romantic love, she realized, wasn't a one–shot deal. There were different levels of romantic love and love itself could be re-

kindled. Doctor Ian Forrester had ignited the tinder in her heart causing sparks to ignite and a new flame to burn within her.

"I love you," he had repeated over and over between lavish kisses in the moonlit garden. He had planted the new seed of love within her heart and soul.

As she lay in the downy warmth of her lumpy mattress, she knew that she loved Ian Forrester. She loved him in that gut–wrenching, spine–tingling deep romantic way. He was a multi–faceted man of intellect and intensity, of sophisticated charm and deep emotion. He was a good person, a loving and patient father, and a gentle lover. When together, sparks ignited. A woman could search a lifetime for such a relationship or go back nearly a century to find the man of her dreams. Modern convenience, technology, medical advances, progress were well and good. Without love, though, all of the inventions, discoveries, and material possessions were meaningless and worthless. Without love, one had nothing. Love is everything.

Faith felt the tears drizzle down her cheeks. Love.

"I do love him, Clarice," Faith mumbled. "I found my one true love."

At breakfast, Bridget noticed a change that was occurring in the Forrester household. Welcome change. She could feel it deep down in her bones and sense it within her heart and soul.

Miss Donahue sat erect and still in her seat. Her face wore the most serene and contended expression. Her eyes sparkled and her complexion had taken on an almost translucent quality.

With one glance at the doctor, seated next to the governess, Bridget knew the reason. The doctor's glistening eyes were trans-fixed on Faith. Though both were unusually silent, a secret con-versation was exchanged with their eyes.

As Bridget leaned down to pour Faith's tea, she wanted to whisper, "I told you so." Instead she smiled and winked. She could have sworn Faith blushed.

Andrew wriggled in his seat, sloshing his spoon in his bowl of porridge. It was clear that he was bored with the silence.

While pouring the doctor's tea, Bridget commented, "The fog's lifted and the sun's brightening up. Bright and beautiful summer morn."

"The most beautiful day of my life," the doctor replied with a dimpled grin.

"Is it now?" Bridget smirked. The doctor kept his eyes glued on Faith as she sipped her tea.

He took a sip of his own tea then set down the cup with a rattle. "I have some news Bridget, Andrew."

Bridget froze in place and Andrew looked up from his bowl.

Doctor Forrester reached over and clasped Faith's hand in his. "Miss Donahue has accepted my marriage proposal."

"Oh, my," Bridget said, acting surprised, though she wasn't. "Good news. Good news, indeed."

She smiled at Faith whose eyes twinkled as she winked and cast a knowing smile her way.

"Is Miss Donahue to be my new mommy?" Andrew asked, leaning over the table.

"Yes."

"Yippee!" Andrew jumped up and down like a jack–in–the–box.

Faith smiled. It was the happiest moment of her life.

"I love all of you so very much," Faith said, holding back tears of joy.

With wishes came tears. Wishes could come true.

After breakfast, Faith supervised Andrew as he played in the back garden. He had become enamored with the Frisbee she had brought him. She had taught him how to fling and retrieve the mysterious flying disc. It provided the boy with entertainment while expelling some of his pent–up energy.

"How many more objects have you in that bag of tricks?" Doctor Forrester asked, hands in his plaid trousers as he sauntered into the garden.

"My backpack's about empty," Faith replied. The best thing she had done was return with the stuffed backpack.

"I certainly hope it isn't your desire to go back for more."

"I can assure, I have no intentions of going back."

"What would we do without you if you did?"

He came up behind her, placing his hands on her shoulders, kneading them with his slender fingers.

"Um, that feels great." He could easily put a masseur to shame, she thought.

He whispered, "You have no idea what great is yet."

"I can't wait." She never thought that a man from the turn of the century could be so sexy.

He nuzzled his face against her neck, nibbled at her ear, and planted kisses on her neck and cheek.

"What will the neighbors say?" she teased.

"That Doctor Forrester is having an illicit love affair with his son's governess."

"Scandalous," she mumbled. His hot kisses were making her flush and tingly.

"More scandalous than the corruption in city hall. Scandalous as in Doctor Forrester marrying his son's governess."

Faith drew away from him, stepping forward and turning to face him. His words and the way he said them gave her pause.

"Faith, Have I said or done something to cause you harm?"

"Doctor," she began.

"Ian, please," he corrected, noting how her expression turned from contentment to contentious and wondering why.

She stepped back, lowering her gaze. Being from another century, the social implications of their marriage hadn't dawned on her. Until now. "Ian, I didn't consider the inappropriateness of our relationship and its social ramifications until now. I keep forgetting my time and place. In 2006, a person could marry whomever he pleased without regard to religion, race, income, or station in life. I keep forgetting, that in 2006, I was a well–respected educator. Here, I am a governess, considered little more than a servant. My intention isn't to create a scandal."

He stepped forward. "I am marrying the woman I love."

"Well and good. Where does that leave me?"

He chuckled. "Dear Faith, I was jesting. In the old San Francisco, I would have been chastised and ostracized for marrying my son's governess. For me it is of little concern. Alas, the fire and earthquake have brought some humility to the city. People have far more to worry about than the local doctor." He reached out to her. "Besides, a little scandal doesn't bother me."

"What am I to do with you?" She shook her head.

"Love me. Just love me." He pulled her into his arms. With one hand against the small of her back and the other around her waist, he pressed her body, molding it against his. They were like pieces of a jigsaw puzzle, the perfect fit.

As his lips met hers, she was consumed by his taste, spicy scent, and intimate touch. Through her heavy skirt, she could feel the length of his manhood pressing against her thigh. She wriggled, wanting him between her thighs, wanting his maleness to perform just as his tongue were prying and exploring in her mouth.

Panting, Doctor Forrester drew back, distancing himself from her body. "Oh, Faith. If we continue, I fear I shall take you right here in the grass. Now, that would be scandalous."

"Ian, take me anywhere. Just take me." She wanted him, all of him, so badly she could scream.

He put his forefinger up to her lips to silence them. "Shh, at the right time, in the proper place. You deserve more from me than a quick romp in the grass."

"I love you," she whispered.

"And I love you. We have a lifetime together." After taking a deep breath, he said, "I must go on my rounds."

"Where are you off to first?" she asked, trying to regain her composure.

"I must visit Mrs. Jamison."

"The ornery old lady with the scared, elderly maid?" Faith asked, remembering how they had shared tea with the headstrong dowager.

"One and the same. Daisy died a few weeks ago."

"I wasn't aware. I'm sorry."

"Mrs. Jamison isn't faring well either, I'm afraid. It seems that her imaginary maladies are becoming all too real. Her body is old and worn. After a while, even the spirit can't keep it alive." He sighed.

Faith thought of own future. She was going to live until age seventy–five. Seventy–five. She would die shortly after the doctor. Would her spirit die with him? She shivered at the thought, rubbing her arms with her hands.

"Faith?" he asked.

"Oh, please send Mrs. Jamison my regards."

"I shall." He turned to leave and glanced back. "And Faith, I meant it about sharing a lifetime together."

Doctor Forrester didn't make it home in time for dinner. By the time his motorcar parked in front, the house was dark. Only the dim gas lamp in the foyer was lit. Andrew was already tucked snugly in his bed. Bridget had gone up to her room for the night. Faith sat awake in her attic room, reading by candlelight. She chastised herself for being like a wife, waiting up with worry over her husband. When she heard the doctor's car sputter to a park, she rushed to the window. She peered out as a weary Ian Forrester slipped out of his vehicle and stumbled up the brick walk.

Donning her flannel robe and slippers, she tiptoed out of her room and down the stairs, using her candle in the brass candlestick for illumination. As the front door opened, she stood on the stairs looking down at the foyer.

Doctor Forrester ambled in, holding a wooden box under his arm. He removed his bowler hat, flinging it on the coat stand. He was about to turn into the library when he saw her.

"Faith?"

She walked down the few remaining steps and met him in the foyer. In the glow of candlelight, his face looked drawn and weary. His shoulders were hunched, his head low. He was working too hard again.

"What are you doing up at such an ungodly hour?" he asked.

"I'm worried about you."

"No need." He wasn't used to anyone worrying about him. It had been so long since anyone really cared, except for Bridget who, at times, was like a mother hen. He looked down at Faith, the golden glow of candlelight washing over her. She looked like an angel standing there, his guardian angel.

"Have you had any supper?" she asked.

"No."

"I'm sure there are leftovers in the fridge."

He arched his brows. "What?"

"Oh, remaining food from supper in the icebox," she translated.

"It's been a difficult day. I'm not hungry. Thank you for being concerned." He yawned.

"I care about you."

"Thank you, Faith." He turned toward the library.

Faith rushed in ahead to light the kerosene reading lamp. As he followed her in, their shadows danced on the illuminated cherry paneling. He set down the box on his desk.

"I'll leave you to your work," she said, turning to leave.

"Don't go," he urged.

She turned to face him. He pointed to his leather swivel chair and she sat.

"The contents of this box concern you more than me. As a matter of fact, I have no idea what's inside. I was ordered to give the box to you," he explained tapping the lid on the box.

"Me? Why? Who is it from?"

"Mrs. Fanny Jamison."

"I hardly know her."

"Apparently, she felt it was important that you have it."

"After seeing what's inside, I'll have to thank her."

"That isn't possible."

"Why?" She had a sudden sinking feeling.

"Fanny Jamison died this evening." He choked on the words. The old woman had meant more to him than he realized. Through the years he had dealt with her various maladies, contrived and real, and a fond affection had grown toward the eccentric dowager. Losing her was like losing a grandmother.

She drew her hands to her face. "Oh, no." Looking up at him, she asked, "You were there?"

He nodded, drawing a deep breath.

"Before she lapsed into her final rest, she begged me to give you the box. She said that only you would understand."

"I'm really quite confused."

"Perhaps you should open the box. I'm as curious as you."

The doctor picked up the polished pine box and set it on Faith's lap. The size and weight of a shoebox, it had a sliding lid. Doctor Forrester leaned on his desk looking down on her.

With some hesitation, she slid open the lid. Eerie chills ran up and down her spine and neck. Knowing that Mrs. Jamison had just died hadn't made the task any easier.

Removing the lid and setting it on the floor, she looked inside. A variety of trinkets, rolled papers and a rolled magazine filled the box.

She stuck her hand inside and pulled out a silver coin. Placing it in her palm, she analyzed it. The recollection made her gasp aloud.

"What is it?" the Doctor asked, squinting for a closer look.

"It's a Bicentennial quarter." She couldn't believe her eyes. *How did Mrs. Jamison get it?*

"A what?"

"A special quarter minted for the U.S. Bicentennial in 1976. They were very common."

With curiosity getting the best of her, she reached in for another object. She withdrew a baseball card.

"I'll be darned," she commented at the sight of a mint Joe DiMaggio collector's card. "This would be worth a fortune."

"What is it?"

She showed the doctor but he didn't understand.

After removing the magazine from the box, she unrolled it. PEOPLE. The cover featured Prince Charles' and Diana's lavish wedding.

"I can't believe it." She was trembling from touching the reminders of her past life. How did Mrs. Jamison get her hands on these things, she wondered?

From the box, she withdrew a plastic American Express credit card. The expiration date was in 1982. The name: Fanella Parker Jamison.

"Oh no! Fanny Jamison was a time traveler. She was just like me. She knew. She somehow knew that we had the experience in common. Why didn't she tell me when she was alive? I would have loved to have discussed it with her."

She turned to look up at the doctor. "You know what this means? I'm not the only person to travel through time. There are others. I'm not some oddball crazy person."

Doctor Forrester looked over the contents of the box. He could offer no explanation. The experience was much like the time when Faith unzipped her strange backpack and revealed its contents. This was another unexplainable Pandora's box. The discovery caused more confusion in his mind, more evidence to support Faith's journey through time.

"There are others like me." The discovery made Faith more at ease with her situation. Others made the journey before her. There were others whose destiny had propelled them back in time, too.

CHAPTER 25

W HILE THE CITY SURROUNDING HER rose from the ashes, Faith began her destined life. Under the rose–entwined arbor at 92 Sacramento Street, she pledged her love and her life to Doctor Ian Forrester.

He stood beside her resplendent in a charcoal frock coat, a stiff collar and a blush rose pinned on his lapel. His face was serene and voice confident as he recited his vows "to love and cherish" her through all the days of his life and beyond. Faith looped one hand through his arm while the other clutched a bouquet of two–dozen blush roses, ivy, and myrtle. The oversized bouquet bobbed up and down mirroring her jitters. Though she looked like a bride in her ivory taffeta and appliquéd lace gown, she couldn't believe that she was getting married. Married. Married again.

When she wed Brad, the ceremony was held in an overflowing cathedral with Mendelssohn, *Ave Maria*, and a Unity candle. Her gown of billowing satin with train and tulle veil required two attendants. She had bridesmaids, groomsmen, confetti, and a horse–drawn carriage. Her father walked her down the aisle and her mother had cried.

A lump formed in her throat. At this simple garden ceremony, there was no one to walk her down the non–existent aisle, no bridesmaids or groomsmen, no organ music, and no one to cry. There was no Clarice and Reggie to share this special moment.

She cast a glance toward Bridget who stood nearby gloating and to Andrew who stood next to his father like a page. In his hands was a velvet pillow supporting two simple gold wedding bands. As the sun's rays illuminated them, the rings shone like magic, as if sprinkled with fairy dust.

The robed minister called her name and Faith looked up. Her eyes caught those of Ian's. Gold specks flickered in his dark eyes as they peered down into hers, deep into her soul. He touched her in places no other man dared to go.

"Repeat after me," the minister began, reciting vows from his prayer book.

After drawing a deep breath of the floral–scented air, Faith said the words binding her heart and soul to Doctor Ian Forrester. This time she knew what marriage and commitment were about. She didn't require all the pomp and pageantry to give herself to Ian. Beneath the floral marriage bell, laden arbor, and under the eyes of God she pledged herself to Doctor Ian Forrester.

This time it was forever.

The wedding breakfast was as traditional as the vows. Bridget prepared the multi–course meal befitting the occasion. The damask covered dining room table was set with the best gold–trimmed china, cut crystal, and sterling. Consommé was ladled from a sterling tureen. Roasted capons with the trimmings provided the main course followed by fresh fruit, bonbons, and tea. A local baker had been commissioned to create the centerpiece, a multi–tiered confection of a wedding cake with almond icing, trimmed with ivory and blush roses.

A photographer had been hired to document the proceedings and to take formal wedding portraits. The acrid scent of flash powder made Faith long for part of modern technology. Nothing modern, though, could compensate for the joy she felt. This was how love was supposed to be. She had to go back through time to experience it.

Faith was glad that she and the doctor had chosen to forgo the public formality of betrothal parties, engraved invitations, guest lists, and receptions. The intimate, family gathering was a more personal statement of their love and the life they would share together.

After tucking Andrew in bed, together, Faith took Ian's hand, interlocking her fingers in his. She led him down the hall to her favorite, familiar bedroom. They passed the stairway leading up to her attic servant's room and entered the guest bedroom, closing the door behind.

The familiar carved mantel, rosewood wardrobe, commode, wicker chair, and white enamel iron and brass bed greeted them, awash in moonlight. To Faith they were like old friends. The bed was where she had awakened into this strange new world. She thought it only fitting that she and Ian would begin their life together in the bed where she had awakened to her future.

Faith turned to Ian, stretching up into him as he bent into her, hips connecting, in an intimate embrace. She reached up, caressing his chiseled face with her hand. Tracing a line from his high cheekbones to his solid square jaw, she pondered his lips. As his eyes melted into hers, like hot chocolate, she pulled his head near hers. He kissed her upper lip first to tease. Tender kisses moved from her face, neck, and eyes to gently brush her mouth and pull at her lips. As she opened her mouth slightly, he took her whole mouth with his flooding her with passionate kisses, his tongue flicking and thrusting. Her eyes closed to savor the moment. Her shoulders softened under his spell as his caressing fingers played with her hair and tingled against her neck. He pulled out the decorative tortoiseshell comb restraining her hair and tossed it on the floor. Releasing her hair in waves of brown, he buried his head in her hair, nibbling at her ear and neck, his breath hot against her flesh.

His hands slid down to the back of her gown, pulling at the seed pearl buttons holding it together. The gown had been almost impossible to secure with Bridget's adept fingers. Faith knew that Ian was struggling. She reached back to help. He drew her hand away. In one sharp movement, the buttons popped as the back of the dress tore open. His caressing hands slid the lace fabric off her shoulders, freeing her arms. He pulled the gown off her hips, letting it flow to the floor in a heap.

She stood in her Wonderbra, pantyhose, and thong panty.

"Oh, my," he murmured, his face blossoming red as his eyes followed her every move.

Faith was certain he never expected to see such a sight on his wedding night. Women of his era wore corsets and wool hose. The body wasn't something one willingly showed off. Sex was more of an obligation than an entertainment. Knowing how ris-qué she must appear, she struck a provocative pose. Arching her back to push out her heaving chest, she placed one foot on the chair and proceeded to slide down her pantyhose, one shapely leg at a time. His eyes grew wide and he stroked beads of perspiration forming on his brow. Tossing the hose on the floor, she sat on the bed, beckoning him with her finger.

He came to her, sitting next to her on the bed. He unbut-toned his frock coat, loosening his necktie and collar. She reached out to help ease him out of the coat, collar, and tie. Jersey knit clung to the curves of his firm chest, neck, and arms. Her fingers caressed his broad chest through the fabric. Reaching up to undo the pearl buttons at his neck, she thrust her hand in the opening, twisting the fine dark hair hidden beneath.

He grasped her fingers, withdrawing them from his shirt's opening. Reaching into his pants, he pulled out the undershirt and yanked it over his head onto the floor.

Faith placed her hands on his bare chest, caressing the taut flesh and silky hair. Her fingers circled each nipple until hard and moved down to the waistband of his pants. With trembling fingers, she undid each button, brushing against the obvious erec-tion covered by jersey drawers. As she touched the pearl buttons, longing to touch his hard flesh, he grabbed her hand. Snickering, he stood to remove his pants and long drawers.

He stood there in all his naked glory watching her as she fidgeted on the bed. In the glow of moonlight, he looked like a Greek statue poised for battle. He went to the bed, leaned over and pushed her into the downy mattress. She lay still as he hovered over her, barely touching.

"It takes two to play this game, Faith," he said. A wicked grin creased his face.

Resting his weight on his elbows, he reached down and kissed her. Forceful kisses gnawed at her lips. Kisses traced a line from her lips to her neck down to the fleshy mounds of her chest. Eyeing the leopard print bra, he hesitated.

"Everything about you is so different," he whispered as his fingers toyed with the silken padded fabric. Grazing her body with his eyes, he traced a line with his fingers from her bra, over her stomach, down to the silky thong panties. She shivered at his intimate touch. He slipped his hand beneath the fabric. Burying his fingers in the curly brown muff, he caressed her, slithering his fingers in her moisture.

Splaying apart her legs, Faith felt like a wanton hussy. She couldn't pretend to be a coy, blushing bride on her wedding night as was expected in the era. She was who she was. Ian seemed to understand it. At least he knew what to do. What he was doing with his gentle fingers was driving her mad. She was hot and flush and tingly. As he positioned himself over her, she touched him. She caressed the tip of his penis, slithering down to stroke the underside and squeeze the base. As he rested on his elbows, she helped ease him into her, filling her. She realized how much she had missed having a man.

Their eyes met with the trust and care only lovers could share. He lowered his head to kiss her as his body began to arch in rhythm with hers. The connection of flesh, the musky scent of damp skin, sharing the same air and space, was complete. He placed his hands on her rounded buttocks, pulling her weight up and down. Up and down. A lover's lullaby. The tension built up until breathing ceased, muscles became rigid, and both simultaneously reached a convulsive, explosive orgasm. Faith arched her back, her face contorted in pleasurable pain. She tingled from her head down to her toes

Ian pulled himself up on his elbows, looking down at her

through glistening eyes. There was something special about the evening, the night their bonding and destiny became complete.

EPILOGUE

THE FOUNDATION FOR SAN FRANCISCO'S Architectural Heritage was proud to show off its newest gem. The Queen Ann Victorian at 92 Sacramento Street, donated by a generous benefactor, made its debut at a private benefit party. Proceeds of the cocktail party and home tour were earmarked for special projects at public schools in the low income Tenderloin district. The Forrester Home, as it was dedicated, was illuminated with gas fixtures and candlelight befitting the early 1900s. Damask table-cloths protected period pieces set with silver trays of scrumptious hors d'oeuvres and delicacies. Baked Brie, dips and crackers, fresh vegetable wedges, smoked salmon, and chilled shrimp provided nourishment for the hundred or so guests meandering throughout the elegantly restored home. White–gloved waiters served cham-pagne on silver trays while a bar offered Chardonnay and Merlot to those so inclined. The mingled scent of food and expensive perfume wafted among the chattering guests.

Clarice stood among the throng, steadying her wine glass in her trembling hand. Being inside Faith's home was like being in a haunted mansion. Without Faith present, the home lacked all of its luster and life. All Clarice had were memories and they were making her nauseous. She wanted to leave and go home to her husband and children. She couldn't, not yet. Her school was a major recipient of the generosity of the foundation and the guests. She had to stand around at the ready to discuss her school and the special projects the money would aid. Discussing literacy and history field trips with society mavens, though, took her mind off of Faith and her mysterious disappearance. When she stood alone, the questions would flood her mind.

Feeling a headache coming on, she sought out a restroom where she could take her aspirin in private. A rather long line formed at the downstairs rest room. Dodging guests, she stepped into the foyer and climbed the mahogany staircase. She knew that there was another restroom off the upstairs hall.

Once upstairs, she noticed that there were few guests. She shook her head. It was typical of a party. Guests tended to gravitate toward the food and the alcohol. She welcomed the quiet respite. Walking down the hall, she passed the guestroom that Faith had treasured. Wasn't it the place where Faith said she had awakened transported back in time? With a quick peek inside, she continued toward the restroom. She abruptly stopped. It felt as if a magnet were drawing her back toward the guestroom. She couldn't shake the urge to turn around and go back to the room. The feeling was so strong that she walked back to the room and stepped inside.

An eerie shiver created goose bumps on her arms and she briskly rubbed them. Light from the streetlamp streamed through the intricate stained glass window giving it a soft glow. The light from a dim glass lamp lent the rosewood wardrobe, dresser and chiffonier warmth. A commode was set with a porcelain toilet set and linen towels as if ready for a guest. Clarice jumped back upon seeing her reflection in the gilt mirror above the carved mantel, a fire flickering in the hearth.

"What is my problem?" she mumbled to herself.

As she approached the white baked–on enamel iron bed, the scent of lavender and lemon verbena prevailed. She reached down to touch the down quilt. As she squeezed the fabric, tears swelled in her eyes.

"Oh, Faith, I miss you so much. You were my soul sister and I love you."

She stood, trying to compose herself. Wiping tears from her

cheeks she turned to leave the room. She had to get out of the room and out of the house before she'd lose it.

"Clarice," a voice beckoned.

Hesitating, Clarice pivoted toward the sound of the hauntingly familiar voice. She gasped, eyes transfixed on the bed, She blinked and blinked again thinking that her eyes were playing tricks on her.

Faith lay beneath the goose down comforter propped up by pillows beneath her back and head. Her brown hair streamed over the pillows and over her narrow shoulders. The lace of a flannel nightgown fit snug at her neck. She smiled and her eyes glistened in vibrant aquamarine.

Clarice swore that the figure on the bed glowed.

"Faith?" Clarice asked, while questioning her sanity at seeing such an apparition.

"I knew you would come. I just knew it," Faith said in an exuberant voice. "I can only stay for a short visit. I just wanted you to know that I'm well and very happy."

"Where are you?" Clarice tried to control her knees from wobbling.

"I succeeded. I made it back to San Francisco in 1906. I'm living in this house. It looks much the same as you see it. I did a rather accurate restoration. I'm proud that others are enjoying it and that your school is benefitting, rather *our* school." She scanned the room and nodded.

"You…you're back in time?" Clarice sunk in the nearby wicker chair.

"I told you I was going back. I've married the doctor."

"The doctor?" Clarice's head was spinning.

"Yes, Doctor Forrester."

"The man in the photograph, the obituary, the cemetery?"

"One and the same. And, we're expecting our child. You know, the little girl you saw in the photograph?" Faith patted her distended abdomen. "Ian has ordered me to bed rest while we await her arrival. I'm naming her Clarice."

"I…I don't believe this."

"Don't you see? It's all working according to plan, according to my destiny."

"Destiny? How did you come back, here and now?" If she had indeed come back and this wasn't some figment of an over-worked imagination.

"I saw you in a dream and I heard you call for me. You were so upset that I willed myself here. I have no explanation. I just think that if you want something bad enough you can will it to happen."

Clarice heard footsteps and looked toward the open door.

"Don't worry," Faith assured. "Only you can see me. I'm invis-ible to everyone else."

"A ghost?"

"Not exactly. I'm just a time traveler on a very short visit. Tell me, how are you my friend?"

Clarice shook her head. "I'm not sure right now."

Faith extended her hand and grasped Clarice's, giving it a gen-tle squeeze.

Clarice gasped at the warmth and energy of the touch.

Faith released her hand. "I brought something back for you."

Clarice met her glassy gaze.

Faith reached under the comforter and withdrew a silver frame. Inside was a sepia–toned photograph of a dapper man and elegant woman on their wedding day. She handed it to Clarice.

Clarice steadied the framed photograph in her trembling hands as she stared at it. There was no mistaking the pair. Doctor Ian Forester stood intimately close with his arm around Faith's waist.

"It's one of our wedding pictures. I really wish that you could have been there. I missed you so." Faith sighed.

Clarice looked at the photograph and at her friend in disbelief. The framed photograph was too real to put off as imaginary.

"I'm happy, really happy. I want you to know that, Clarice. I don't want you shedding tears for me. I'm where I was meant to be."

"Oh Faith, Faith, I miss you."

Their eyes locked.

"I love you Clarice. I'll always love you. I'll always miss you."

Clarice reached out to touch Faith but she was gone. The comforter lay smooth and unruffled on the bed, the pillows positioned in their rightful places at the head of the bed. The scent of lavender and lemon verbena had drifted away.

"Faith?" Clarice stood and reached out over the bed, running her hand on top. The surface was cool and untouched like a bed–and–bath store display. There was no evidence that a person had lain on it.

She looked down realizing that she still held the framed photograph in her other hand. She looked at the smiling couple in the old picture. Doctor and Mrs. Ian Forrester. Faith Forrester. Faith. The photograph was the only evidence that something unexplainable had taken place.

ABOUT THE AUTHOR

Purveyor of the written word, Nancy Loyan Schuemann has been writing ever since she began composing picture books for fellow students in elementary school.

After graduating with a BSBA degree in marketing from John Carroll University, she pursued a career in sales and marketing. She has incorporated those skills into a career as a multi-published freelance writer and author.

Nancy is a Cleveland, Ohio native who shares her knowledge of the city as author of

Cleveland, Ohio: A Photographic Portrait and *On the Threshold of a New Century: The City of South Euclid, 1967-1999.* Her love, however, is writing women's fiction. Her novels include *Paradise Found, Lab Test, Hearts of Steel, Wishes and Tears, The Right Combination. Special Angel, Champagne for Breakfast,* and *A Kiss in the Rain.* She has also taught writing at the Chautauqua Institution and Cuyahoga Community Public Library.

Travel has taken her around the country and around the world, including trips to the Caribbean, Europe, Great Britain, South America, Egypt and the exotic Seychelles Islands. When she's not writing, Nancy teaches and performs, Middle Eastern dance as "Nailah" (www.NailahDance.com) She shares her life with her husband, Bill, and her fur children Pointer/Labs, Amber and Topaz.

Her web site is www.NLSScribe.com

44342723R00118

Made in the USA
Middletown, DE
04 June 2017